See Ya

By Cheryl Kerr

For Meghan and Loren
and
children everywhere

Chapter 1

July 4, 1996

The Fourth of July dawned hot and bright and blue. We were giving a party that afternoon, Cameron and I, under the oak trees that stood sentinel in the back yard of our new home.

The gathering would be a celebration of several things. We had just bought this house from my parents, Matthew and Ginny; an article had just come out that mentioned Matthew; and there was just plain catching up to do with old friends.

We rose early that morning to ready tables and chairs under streamers hung from fat oak branches, stack plates and cups, and fill ice chests with drinks against the heat.

At 8:00 a.m. I broke for a moment from wrestling a picnic table into place and leaned back against the limestone wall of the house. My skin was already moist and I pushed my hair from my forehead with an impatient hand.

The house breathed out the curious cool that thick stone walls hold even in the worst summer heat. This house was built in 1869, in the days when Austin was first settled. The limestone blocks were rough-hewn and chunky. Inside, the rooms were dim. And silent, as if within them time stood still.

I looked down the long sloping back yard to the creek at yard's end and took a deep drink from my cup of water.

The oak trees lay heavy pools of shade, branches stirring, streamers and tablecloths fluttering gently in the faint breeze. Beyond them, creek water winked in the sunlight. The red, white and blue decorations were a standard Fourth of July theme, but in this case they also honored Matthew's thirty years of Air Force service.

He had been the focal point of a story about his Pentagon days published just the week before in *Stars and Stripes*. Once he had been a full colonel, admired and well-spoken of. People still kept track of him.

Now in town by chance for a unit reunion, many had called, and the party went from little to big in nothing flat, the way many of our happenings do.

I looked around our yard. We had only recently moved in, and we were a long way from House Beautiful material. It would be Matthew and Ginny's first time as guests here. They had moved into this house more than twenty years ago, when Matthew came back to Texas after long tours with the Pentagon.

The two of them were full of plans these days, new condo owners delighted with having nothing to do but shut the door and go. They were ready to travel light at last, it seemed.

I went back to work, and the morning sped by.

At eleven the doorbell began to ring, and by noon people were gathered in chairs scattered around in two groups, one beneath the live oaks and pecan trees that edged the creek and another near the chips and drinks on the porch.

The heavy scent of citronella lay over the party, keeping the mosquitoes at bay. Voices grew into a hum, laced with the sounds of laughter and old rock and roll from the CD player someone had switched on.

At noon Cameron lit the grill for burgers and took a head count for the first batch, his familiar long length wreathed in smoke. Our girls flitted in and out between him and everything he was trying to do. Our oldest, Linnea, at seven, was barely ribcage-high when she got right up next to him and determinedly tried to match his stride and reach as he moved and set things out.

From inside I watched and smiled and kept putting things together. After twelve years, I still liked to look at him. Linnea and Leah both had Cameron's hazel eyes and my brown hair. They were saddle-tan, hair sun-streaked, so that they looked like a play of moving light and shadow even when they were standing still, which was almost never.

The door opened and Ginny came inside. My mother and I looked nothing alike. I was dark and slender, like the Indian great-grandmother I had, sharing even her dark, dark eyes. Ginny was slender, had high cheekbones and wore her frosted bob tucked behind her ears. She did not ask if I needed help, just glanced at what I had done and went to the fridge for the trays of tiny quiche we had prepared the night before.

She was competent, quick and self-sufficient, the essence of Air Force wives who juggled households for months on end when husbands were gone. Ginny carried on that "do-it-myself" mannerism even when Matthew came home. They made a team but moved independently of each other.

And what about Cameron and me? I tried to decide while I refilled my glass with iced tea. I wasn't sure, but before I could take the thought further, three-year-old Leah burst into the room, crying. Behind her, the screen door slammed with a crack, a sound that always called summer to me.

"Her won't let me be outside!" she pointed indignantly to Linnea, who entered behind her, rolling her eyes. Leah's lower lip stuck out in a pout, and her eyes brimmed with unshed tears, the picture of misery and suffering. Mad at her big sister. At three all she wanted to be was what Linnea already was. That made her older sister a star to reach for, one that burned when it reached down from its great height and told the little sister "no."

"Okay." I dropped into the kitchen rocking chair and pulled Leah into my lap, shifting my iced tea as I settled her weight. The ragged breathing slowed enough that she could explain that Linnea was getting in her way while she tried blowing bubbles through the smoke from the hamburger fire. I held her, heavy on my shoulder, and peered out the window to see how people were doing.

Cameron waved a spatula that the first burgers and toasted buns were ready. And Matthew, laughing, was the first in line at the grill, taking a patty from the burgers heaped at one end. He turned to sit down and simply sank to the ground. The move was oddly slow and graceful, like a dancer at the end of his performance. But Matthew had never been a dancer.

I rocked and waited, my daughter in my arms. But he didn't move again. I remember feeling the icy glass sliding through my fingers as I watched him lying oh so still. I do not recall putting Leah down, or moving from kitchen to yard.

The next thing I knew I was beside him.

"Matthew - Dad," I said, kneeling. But he didn't answer, and in the sudden hush I heard someone calling for an ambulance, the words far off and tinny-sounding to my ear. Cameron pushed me to the side and tore open Matthew's shirt, already counting for CPR. Someone else held Matthew's head steady and echoed Cameron's cadence.

I stayed there, my father's hand in mine, until the sirens shrilled to a stop at our door. The other voice went on calling when to breathe and not. I recall watching Cameron raise his head and say "Matthew, come on." Ginny was there, too, kneeling beside us, calling Matthew's name in a high keening cry.

I only remember the rest in bright and vivid flashes.

Heart attack, they said; nothing more they could do there - he needed to be transported at once, already sprouting tubes, covered in blankets and attended by urgent murmurs. And so we went.

A flash-forward of pulsing lights and sirens, Ginny and I were at the emergency room with cold steel and tile and Matthew quiet on a table.

Somewhere between one second and the next, faint breathing became final stillness - one moment, breath drawn, and then not another. I do not remember why, but suddenly everyone was gone and it was just Matthew and me in that cool and silent place. Ginny had gone down the hall with the preacher. I could hear her, her voice climbing, wound up tighter and tighter, refusing the calming words.

Matthew, I willed. But no breathing answered my wishes, my prayers for my father on the table. I watched the clock on the wall make its slow way on to each second. I kept thinking that I could make it one more count without screaming, but oh, they were so slow. Tick…tock…tick…tock.

In the faraway place that is reality, I thought, *so this is it. This is dying*. But I really didn't believe. In my sandals and shorts I kept looking at him, kept wondering just when the soul wafts away. In so visible a person, a character so strongly felt, how could it not be seen when it went on its way?

****

Colonels' families live at the ever-ready, as Matthew had said a lot in my years of growing up, and must always be prepared. I dug deep, back into that childhood training in that moment of my father passing and my mother's grief. I gulped in air and I could feel tears hot and tight in my throat. *Soldiers do not cry*, echoed in my head.

I knew that if I started, I would not stop. So I stood, chilled in my summer clothes, and felt life shift around me. That day it seemed to me all things should stop.

But they didn't, not the clock in the emergency room ticking away the moments he no longer knew as time, nor the sounds of people in the hall beyond my cold and quiet room. Around us, the hospital and beyond it, life hummed on. Planes flew, phones rang and people cried.

Surely it was a bad dream from which I would wake any moment and find my world the way it had been. Summer coming and Cameron and Matthew and Ginny and my kids. Summer, easy and sweet and warm and known.

I could not look at the room, watching instead the reflection of us in the polished steel cabinets that banked the walls, as though that made being there less real.

A nurse came in with papers on a clipboard and a doctor in tow. She wore turquoise scrubs with a purple name tag that said "Ruth". The doctor was thin and young and rumpled, with mousy brown hair, a white coat and chinos.

"We need you to identify the...him," the doctor said, changing his words when he saw me flinch at the anticipated word. *Body*. At the rawness of this time.

I swallowed hard and whispered, "That is my father."

"I'm sorry, but we need his full name." The doctor looked, if possible, even more miserable than my own wavy image reflected in the cabinet of instrument trays. Behind him, the nurse worked busily with her neat pages.

"That is Matthew J. Rankin," I said. The doctor looked relieved, wrote it down and held the clipboard out for my signature. I scrawled my name, Manda Carlson, and he took back his forms and pushed fast out the swinging door with the nurse at his heels. Job complete.

I stood for moments longer, I don't even know how many, and at last I nodded to myself. That was Matthew, my father, who had died and now it was time for me to go. I passed into the waiting room where Cameron found me and drove Ginny and me home.

I felt strange and suspended. As if no burial would happen, no grief would engulf, that surely any moment I would waken and this would not be real. We put the girls to bed and made a pot of coffee, black and strong enough to scald resolve into us with each sip.

Over floral decorated mugs we sat at the round polished dining room table and watched the wind pick fitfully at the forlorn streamers and paper plates laid out just that morning.

I moved to take Ginny home, but she raised a quick hand and said, "Cameron." I stopped short, blinking hard, and she explained, "He doesn't cry." I nodded, stung, and stood watching as he helped her into our Jeep, watched as the red tail-lights disappeared around the corner.

I was alone. I looked out the dark windows. Eternity looked back.

Two Days Later

Burying day. I awoke early, lying quietly in the darkness. To the east lay sunrise and the cemetery. Beside my ear the clock flipped its digital numbers, and each click brought me one measure closer to today's 2:00 p.m. ceremony.

All days have the same parts, dawn and dusk, hours and minutes and seconds. On this morning, this one day only in forever, I thought, dawn's fingers will find and sunbeams will light the sharp edges of the new dug grave, moving across corner and side from one end to the other.

Perhaps, I thought, I should go to see its emptiness. But I knew somewhere deep inside me that looking at a hole would not tell me where Matthew was.

Instead, I lay in the silence and thought of 2:00 p.m. on other afternoons. If I stayed in bed, would the cool sheets keep today at bay? Would this 2:00 p.m. not come if I didn't throw them back, if I pretended that today wasn't real? Things are different in the night, closer and intimate, the immensity of unknowns and mutterings is there, but still hidden by the dark.

I braved up, slid from beneath the sheets and dressed quickly. In the kitchen I turned on one light, making coffee by its yellow glow. While the water gurgled and wheezed into the coffeemaker, I leaned one hip against the counter and took in the room.

Today I would leave its familiar lines and lengths and shadows to go and bury my father. And the things that had been the same would never be so again. The spaces of doors and lights and windows would still be there - it was I who would be different. No, I already was.

For two days I had felt suspended, caught in the cottonwool of disbelief, a softness that I could not see or feel through, like being wrapped in clouds. I kept thinking that in a minute the whiteness would part. I would wake from this dreamy state and move back into the world. My world.

Cameron and the girls slept on, and I welcomed the chance to be alone. Over the past two days they had given me space and hugs. I had wakened this morning to see Cameron alone at the window, listening to an owl's hooting. Just once he had raised a hand and wiped an eye, carrying his own sadness so that I would not have to.

But it was not so. The phone began to ring, and then the doorbell, and at eleven I went to take my shower and get ready for the funeral.

The girls were easier, open tears and ragged breathing, things I could see and fix with a glass of chocolate milk.

Thank goodness, I thought, that my own children did not carry on with my own solitary way of grief.

****

When I was little, high summer's 2:00 p.m. was the time of day when all living things were still and heavy in the heat. Even the cicadas paused strumming their pulsing song that clocked the afternoon's time.

It was the hour of day in childhood that seemed to bring the minutes to a stop, as though they were too stuck with sweat to move, too damp and limp to get lifted by any breeze, glued in place by the bright, hot sun.

In those days when time paused, the shadowy interiors of grapevine caves beckoned, dim and cool. The heavy vines hung like curtains from the branches of oaks and cedars in our yard, and you could push through and find veritable rooms inside.

They were our own mansions, for make-believe and adventure and the dreams of years to come.

But then the cicadas began their summer song again, and the shimmer of sounds made the stillness tremble slightly, and the seconds would quake and shiver and begin their march once more, as they have on all the summer afternoons ever since, bringing us to now.

****

We were almost late for the funeral. I had not been able to choose a dress, I did not have many and nothing fit right that day. Cameron didn't know what to do with Leah, her silent objection and willful tears as he tried to get her ready.

"Want Mama," came her tiny, fretful voice.

But we got there just before two and took the last spot right next to the sidewalk. *Family*, I read on a small scripted sign at its front.

"What," I wondered out loud to Cameron, "happens if the grieving aren't family members?"

"Manda." He sighed. "Let's go."

We bustled out of the car and Cameron swung open the chapel door for me. Just inside, in the small vestibule, Ginny and my brother, Sam, waited. Ginny looked relieved at our entrance. She looked us over, then she and Sam each took one of the girls' hands and went down the aisle. Cameron did the same, but instead of moving forward I rested back against his hand, refusing to walk into the dark from the bright day's light. I wiped beads of sweat from my lip.

This was an entering I did not want to make; it was far too symbolic, walking from light into dark.

I stayed rooted, and the organ music began a second run through, a little louder this time. A hint for the errant family member to come please, now, to the front of the church. We have someone to bury.

Cameron's hand tensed in the small of my back and he propelled me into the church. The gloom swam and settled before my eyes into pews and people and the casket set in the sunbeam pouring through the stained glass window just above the altar. In the front pew Ginny and my brother Sam were already seated, watching and waiting.

We started past people turned in their seats, craning to see who was coming. Faces were pale moons with features my gaze took in but did not see, as I looked to the front of the church.

"See ya." The words were so clearly spoken in my ear that I wheeled in the midst of a step, pulling away from Cameron's hand to turn and stand stock-still, staring back toward the heavy door.

Matthew used those words to me, me alone, long ago when my latter childhood years were a rocky trip for us both. I had not heard them since.

As if a sign, the doors closed with a muffled thump, shutting out the hot brightness and keeping in the shadows and grief and sorrow.

Cameron met my eyes with worry in his own, put his hand on my elbow again, harder this time, and we moved on up the aisle.

The two little words had been Matthew's shorthand casual way of leaving. But he had always come back. Before.

I focused on the steps I needed to take.

With every footfall the grief of the past two days rose higher in my throat.

Dimly I realized the church was filled. The drill weekend that had made so many able to make our party had kept them here for his goodbye. The practices of the reserve army and Air Force units that were Matthew's career and group for over thirty years had made him lifelong friends.

Cameron handed me into the first pew beside Sam and settled the girls between us. I slid then from mother to sister, feeling my brother standing tall and silent, as unable to speak his grief as I. A long trip from his home in Georgia had brought him in just this morning. His face wore the soft, confused look of a small child upon waking, and I felt an ages-old spasm of protectiveness for my little brother. I could pick on him, but others did not dare.

His gaze didn't leave the coffin, and, beyond him, Ginny also stood face front and at attention. And the service went on around us.

Matthew was a soldier. A soldier's soldier, they said in his eulogy that used the words printed just a few weeks before in the pages of *Stars and Stripes*. A man committed to his principles and his country, as though those are the same thing.

At the graveside, planes swept low overhead against the same hot blue sky that only two days before had been the canvas for our party. I watched them go, hearing the minister intone about going home and the twenty-one guns saluting.

Overhead the vapor trails spread lazily outwards like an angel flexing its wings. Then sweat clouded my vision and the next thing I knew we were going back to our house.

Cameron drove. I sat silently next to him, one side of my face cold from the air conditioning, the other hot from the sun. I thought about the words breathed in my ear that morning. *See ya.*

Who knows why some words stick in our minds? Fragment or phrase or tag lines of words that once were uttered. Like a snatch of a song or the vivid photoflash of a moment. Some things do not go away.

At our house at last, an easy walkup supper of ham and coffee and cake brought the closest of those we knew. More tears and hand pressing took me to the end of my strength, and I sank into a corner chair, letting the guests swirl on without me.

I watched my mother and could not fathom her reserve.

She looked stretched, skin taut over bone as she moved from guest to coffee to door. But she never quit moving. I had not seen her look like this since the time Matthew had scrambled for a fighter pilot readiness exercise and one of the planes went down.

That day the infirmary was called to send an ambulance. Ginny was on duty. She took the transmission of who the pilots were. Matthew was one of them. Protocol demanded the nurse on duty go. She did, not knowing if he was dead.

Matthew always said that he went up to check the status of the response crews, how ready they were to handle the emergencies that sometimes needed his attention.

It was sometimes that, I think, but also because it was an adrenalin rush, a guy thing to do. Matthew liked those things. I knew that about him, but also that toughness kept anything else inside. Matthew didn't ever really go off duty, never put aside that readiness in his role as a family man.

He survived the crash, never expecting that we would do less than deal with the fear of his dying.

It was that handling whatever came along that toughened us into the non-expression of fear and grief that froze my own tears now.

I looked around the living room and saw how many of Matthew and Ginny's group had come. I smiled and nodded and pretended to listen to the words and memories of all those present.

I thought it did not seem possible so much could happen in a few days' passing. Then mercifully, the gathering was over. Plates put down, kisses given, hands pressed, and the doorbell at last silenced.

Then there was only the going on.

I said goodnight to Ginny, embracing her at the last minute. She slid like a shadow from my arms, giving me a brief look as she went out into the night. Cameron drove her home again. This time I didn't ask. Instead I cleaned up late into the night, trying to scrub and wash away the ebb and flow of the funeral and the dark.

Chapter 2

July 9, Goings and Comings

My fingers crept up toward the phone yet again, stopped and returned once more to rest in my lap. My mother had not answered her phone in the two days since Matthew's funeral service. Had not called me either, though I had wished for her to.

But, if I were honest, the real reason I had not called again was that I did not know how, really, to bridge the chasm that emotion was for my family.

I had been a shy and unsure child, skittery, made more so by the moves to each Air Force base when Matthew got his latest assignment. Among the bluff and blustery people so good at newness, I had drawn tight inside myself, knotted by the conflict of childhood needs and the culture of "stand up straight, soldier."

In that world, we, in our family, no less than others, learnt to fight our own battles, to not whine, to not lean upon one another. We became the solitary, transient people that the service so often bred.

And so, true to my history, I had excused myself from calling Ginny more than a perfunctory amount the whole of the day before. Too early, too late, too soon.

But this morning, the third after the funeral, dawned cool and clear, unheard of in our July days. This day, I told myself, I would do the reaching I was so hesitant about.

I picked up the phone and dialed my mother's number again. And still got no answer, only Ginny's voice on the recorder: *leave a message and we'll call you back at our earliest convenience.* I did not wait, but drove to buy bagels and coffee and then headed for their condo.

It had a tight, shuttered look as I pulled up and turned off the engine. The curtains were completely drawn and two newspapers lay tucked on the single step to the door. I rang first and then jangled my key in the lock as loud as I could to announce my coming. Trying to respect the space and time of grief, but worried.

The lock clicked and I swung the door open. There Ginny stood, in jeans and a crisp white blouse, with two suitcases at her feet. Her hair was tucked back and she wore the hoops she referred to as her "travel earrings."

She looked startled, guilty and disappointed in a fleeting run of expressions. The coffee grew uncomfortably hot in my fingers and I set it down on the hall table. The cups steamed gently and fogged the mirror hung there, just a bit at the very bottom.

"Manda," she said and sighed. "You brought breakfast."

"Yes," I said.

"Let's have a cup of tea instead," she said, and I sensed uneasiness. Ginny had always made tea when something was amiss.

I followed her to the kitchen. She ran water into the teakettle, then put it on to boil. I slid onto a stool at the bar and waited. I loved this room. The back of their new condo faced east and now Ginny moved to open the back door so that sunlight fell in a bright wave across the countertop and the sounds of a squirrel's scolding came in with the cool morning air. She moved back to the counter and laid both her hands flat on its surface in front of her and stared fixedly down at them.

She sighed again. "I hoped to go before you got here. I wrote a note for you." She tilted her head at a piece of paper lying on the counter in between us, as though it would explain and pacify and make all things well.

"Why don't you tell me, since I'm here," I said.

"Well, you know we were supposed to leave on a trip. Today." She looked down again. Almost as if she expected her hands to do a magic trick and make one of us disappear.

I watched her. They had been heading for the Bahamas - beaches and good food.

Ginny spoke to her fingers. "I have to get out of this town," she said. "I just cannot, right now, stand to be here. So I am going to take a trip."

"I see," I said carefully, trying not to react. So now I looked out into the green, cool morning and thought.

Yesterday, while I worried about calling, she had been phoning and planning and packing. Ginny had, as was frequent in her life, kept her own counsel and made her own decisions. Grief would keep us each to ourselves it seemed. We would not sit and share.

Outside a horn tooted. "Darn," my mother said. She flicked her wrist to check the time. And looked at me again. On the stove the teapot began to gather its whistle. "I'll ask him to wait for half an hour. That will be cheaper than calling him back." I nodded. Half was better than none. Her shoes tapped away to make this work.

While she was gone, I fixed tea in the thick mugs that were good to wrap your hands around when they were cold. Mine were cold right then.

Ginny came back and perched on a new, blond barstool and told me about her trip.

"I could not go to all those places we had planned to see together and wonder what he would have thought."

I nodded. "That makes sense."

"So the travel people thought, too," she replied. "They were sorry but the best they could do was trade one trip for another, space available, of course."

"Where are you going?" I asked.

"To Australia, for six weeks. All flights, hotels, meals, and tips already arranged and paid for. All I have to do is meet the plane tonight. In Los Angeles. I have to leave soon to catch my LA flight from here."

It probably was better than sitting still. Ginny looked up just then, as though hearing my thoughts and said, "Right now I just can't take care of anyone beyond myself." For a moment she looked me full in the eye, then her gaze fluttered and dropped.

The horn honked again and she gathered her purse and slung a case to her shoulder. "I hope you are all right with this. It seems that I waited for so long. And I feel so out of control. We made plans, so many plans. And I just cannot stay here and think about all those plans that didn't happen. All the plans that will not ever happen now." She paused. "There's a key and a number, for emergency use."

My gaze followed hers and I saw them on the hall table, right next to the cooling cups of coffee.

I slid off the stool and gathered her other suitcase in my hand. I noticed then that both cases were the flowered ones Ginny had always used. A bit of her past would go with her on all the stops of this journey. Was it on purpose, or had she just forgotten the new luggage she and Matthew had just bought?

"We better get you outside," I said. And with a quick kiss, she was gone as I handed in her into the cab, squinting against the sun.

In the summer, heat gets in the way of seeing, sears your vision until everything is washed and paled by the glare of the light and the heat haze. I went back inside, and the silence flowed around me like water about a rock. Deep within I felt the quivering of the long-ago-little-child-me and suddenly I wanted my mother, with her cool hands and a Band-Aid on this biggest hurt of all.

I sat and finished my tea, rinsed my cup and locked up the home of my parents who were suddenly both gone.

And Pieter Begins His Search

But into every empty dimple in life, something flows. About the time Ginny was relaxing into her first class seat with hot jasmine towels for her face and chilled white wine at hand, another passenger was winging his way on a journey of his own. We did not know, but we were his destination.

Chapter 3

July 11, Pieter Arrives

P ieter Becker first came to my door, so recently Matthew and Ginny's, on a day when I was already stirring the past, sweeping and scrubbing as though I could wipe away grief like dust from a tabletop.

That morning was fragmented by disruptions, both my own and other people's. When I am unhappy I wind tight into myself and grow tense with all I think I alone must do.

I was shuffling out the reminders and souvenirs of Matthew and Ginny's life, many of them from my childhood. Good things, but there were so many of them, each one nudging recall. Matthew and Ginny had taken only what would fit in the condo when they moved. The rest was still here, to be gone through later by all of us. But Matthew's death had changed that.

In any house there must also be room for the life that is now, and it was up to us to make that space. Each thing I would pick up to pack triggered a memory as clearly as if it were projected on a screen in front of me.

Matthew's collection of Miss Marple paperbacks. I had bought them one by one as I found them in used bookstores or estate sales. As his heart slowed, my bringing him books became a moment of surprise in a string of quieting days. I ran my finger over the limp yellow tag yet stuck on one, $1, worth far more than that price.

A photograph of Cameron's and my wedding day, the shot of Matthew walking me up the aisle, handsome as ever in his dress whites and a host of medals. We are looking at each other, smiling. It reminds me that my best times with Matthew were always these sudden moments, the ones that lay halcyon bright in my mind.

And tucked way back in the corner of a pocket shelf was the first clay horsehead I ever made. Angular and oddly cocked, it looked back at me, even now, a horse. Many years after that try at artwork my most-loved mare, Skye, tilted her head in just such a way when she was trying to please me.

My rememberings were pinpricks of sharpness, a few spots crystal clear, and around them the rest of the picture softly fuzzy. I vaguely knew Cameron came twice to the doorway, but I kept to my solitary task.

The rumble of an engine cut into my reverie and, with a guilty start, I looked up at the paint-spattered clock radio squatting against the far wall. Ten o'clock. I had whiled away the first part of my day.

Behind me walls and floor lay bare and scrubbed clean in the daylight. I had worked as though the more I rubbed, the more clearly I would understand Ginny's decision to go on her trip. In the garage was a mounting pile of things for keeping.

They did not fit my life, but who was I to discard the treasures of another? I had spoken to my mother when she called from LA the day before. *Did she want them in storage, to go through once she was back?*

"No," her voice wavered on the airport phone. "No, I'll be okay with whatever you decide to do. I trust your judgment on what to keep. I had enough trouble just deciding on what to bring for this trip."

I had taken the receiver away from my ear and stared at it. We were not talking about her taking these things on a trip. A surge of grief and resentment crested. Why was I the one left to sort and pack forty years of memories?

Now I heard voices, familiar ones, and my mother-in-law stepped in.

"Morning," Doll said, stepping over boxes and a stack of old newspaper to kiss my cheek. Behind her Benton Carlson loomed in the doorway, as tall and spare as his son, a man who does more than he says. I kept Doll's hands in mine and looked askance at their arrival.

"The kids," said Cameron from behind me. "I thought summer should bring some time with Granny and Grandpa."

I looked at the girls behind him in the hall and my conscience twinged. *Yes, I have been gone inside myself. Little faces should not be puckered in worry, eyes round with concern for me.* I nodded. "Go, they should," I said. Leah's face broke into a huge smile and she gripped her stuffed Tigger even more firmly than she hugged my knees. Then in a flurry of suitcases and I love you's, we walked them to the car. Bent's Dodge whined, and I watched them pull away, a craggy rancher, his tiny wife and two bits of my heart. By noon they would be pulling into the family ranch along the bluegreen Blanco River west of Austin. And there, waiting, would be hotdogs and Patches, the aged and childwise gelding whose mother had been my own mare, Skye.

I went back inside, and the house was silent around me. Cameron was working outside. Everyone was trying to give me space. But space for me that day was not easy breathing room; instead it came from inside me, a huge edge of darkness that I teetered on like a tightrope artist walking above a chasm.

Then the doorbell rang.

I opened the door, expecting to find a delivery person with the sandwiches we had ordered for lunch. But at the curb was a yellow taxi, engine running. A man stood on the porch, blond, pressed and neat, dressed just enough differently that I sensed he was from away. He had the bluest eyes I had ever seen, like the clearest of skies on a cool autumn day.

"Yes?" I said, as I leaned against the doorframe and tried to straighten the bandana that held back my hair. My visitor nodded back at me, polite and mannered, not letting on that he noticed my messy self.

"Good morning." He gave a small, formal bow from the waist. "I am looking for Matthew Rankin's house," he said in precise, flavored English. "Is this the address?"

"It was. Yes," I said; *still is, somehow*, my heart murmured.

"I traveled over to see him," he said.

My stomach clutched and I drew a deep breath to steady myself. Would it get easier to do? This telling?

"We lost him a few days ago," I said, wondering at how we come to use so many words for unalterable things.

"Excuse?" He frowned slightly. "Lost him?"

"He's at the cemetery," I said.

"Oh, did someone die? My condolences," he bowed slightly again. I looked at him and thought, he doesn't know. Not everyone does.

"Yes," I said, "Matthew did."

"Matthew Rankin died?" His voice went higher, the way a child's does when the answer isn't what they want to hear.

"Yes. I'm sorry," I said, wondering why I felt the need to apologize. I did want my visitor to leave so I could finish my task.

But he stood there still and looked at me as if there were something I could do for him. I sighed inside, tired of helping people, of knowing answers about bodies and services, of tears and memories.

"Did you know him?" he asked me then.

"Yes," I answered, "He was my father."

"Is your mother perhaps around?"

"No, she isn't here either." I heard the harshness of my words, and the silence that fell flat after them, leaving both of us just standing at a door at noon.

Cameron's boots sounded on the tile behind me, and then his hand pressed into the small of my back.

"Manda?" He frowned slightly as his eyes met mine and slid on by to the man on the porch. He held out a hand to our visitor. "Cameron Carlson." He nodded.

Our visitor offered a slim hand in a brief shake.

"Pieter Becker." We all looked at each other for a moment that stretched longer and longer.

Cameron said to the man, "We buried Matthew a few days ago. I'm sorry for your trouble in coming."

"And I for your loss." Still Pieter Becker hesitated. He turned halfway to go and then swung back and proffered a picture to Cameron. "I do not wish to bother, but I have come a very long way."

Cameron took it and looked for a moment. Then he held it out so I could see too. I moved closer, feeling regret at my sharpness. It would only take a minute to look. I dropped my eyes to the image. It was a shot of two men in a crowded station in front of a swirl of people.

One of them was Matthew, the other a face I did not know.

Without a word I handed the photo back to him. Cameron saw that this bit and piece of memory was too much for me right now. He looked again at Pieter, at those blue, blue eyes.

"Better come in," he said, and stepped back to pull the door open. As he waved his cab away and stepped inside, our visitor was backlit by the sun and passed into our home in darkened silhouette. I felt a frisson run finely along my skin, a shiver that swept through and then was gone. A sense of having seen that figure before, either as premonition or déjà vu, but I could not say which.

Cameron ushered Pieter into our back room, cool with tile and a ceiling fan. I went to rinse my face in the bathroom down the hall and heard iced tea being offered as I patted myself dry. I looked at myself in the mirror and sighed. Not one of my better days.

Many people were still stopping by to pay their respects, coming here because it was my parents' last known address. He and Ginny hadn't yet had time to send out cards announcing their move to the condo.

But these people were catching us unawares. I had a private self and a public one, and I needed space between the two. We tried to always be hospitable, to listen, especially since Ginny was not here. But I was about remembered out.

It seemed the more I listened to reminiscences, the more I could not recall the man we had buried. The stories were flat, like a script to a show in which I knew neither characters nor plot.

Now I made a face at my reflection, pushed my hair back and went to join them, ready to listen once more. I found Cameron in our big rocker and Pieter Becker sitting neatly on one end of the couch. He was slim, with the high cheek-boned face that can be almost any age. I sank into the other end of the sofa and sipped my own glass of tea that Cameron had thoughtfully made for me. Cameron sat rocking gently and listening to Pieter. He said mildly, "We were just chatting about Matthew." But his eyes held mine for a minute longer. You might want to hear this, they seemed to say.

"Okay," I said.

Pieter turned to me, resting his hands loosely on his knees.

"I think your father knew mine, maybe."

"Oh?" I asked him, glancing at Cameron.

"I do not know for sure. I did not know my own father. But, see." He pulled a brown envelope from his satchel. The paper edges were worn to fuzzy folds and the flap corners bent and soft from many uses. He opened it again and placed three pictures side-by-side on the table in front of me with a soft slap, as though he were laying out cards.

He gave me a moment to view them, and then he drew our attention to the one on the left, a group shot of men in baggy pants and flat-brimmed caps. Old-fashioned clothes. The picture was black and white, the faces tiny ovals with eyes and lips and noses that could actually be made out. At the bottom was written a short name and number of the group.

With an index finger he singled out a man on the bottom row. "That man is my father."

"Okay," I said. It must have been taken long ago, for the man in the picture was far younger than the son who sat next to me now.

The next picture was a staff shot of my father. Head and shoulders, straight gaze and eagle insignia in a picture I knew at once. Ginny had it on her bedroom wall; it was Matthew's last official photograph, taken just before his active duty tour ended in 1975 at Kenneth Air Force Base on Cape Cod.

"A man I just met says he saw this man," his finger touched gently on his father's face in the battalion shot, "with this man." His finger moved to Matthew's.

Matthew's picture had been taken with hundreds of troops. That was not an unusual thing. But then he had said he did not know his father. I had the uncomfortable feeling Pieter had followed my every thought. That he had patiently been waiting for me to catch up with him before he moved on.

"And then there is this picture," he took up the one he had shown me at the door. Matthew and a man in front of a blur of people, both looking like they did not want the picture to be taken. But caught in the moment all the same.

He brought a magnifying glass from his satchel and held it over the first picture in the row. He ran it slowly along the small line at the bottom until the numbers and letters grew clear and white in the eye of the glass.

"Please to read those numbers," he requested and waved toward the picture of the group of men. I bent over and read. "Soissons, France, Third Armory. May 18, 1944."

I stared at him, puzzled. What did this have to do with Matthew? The pictures were obviously taken decades apart. During World War II Matthew had been a teenager on the streets of New York, site of leavings and homecomings and victory parades with ticker tape confetti. I could not see a connection.

Cameron moved to stand beside me. "I think it might help if you go back a bit and tell us what brought you here."

Pieter stood and took off his coat, folding it carefully beside him before he sat back down. It seemed this story would take some telling. I curled my legs up beneath me as Pieter began. Above us the ceiling fan continued its somnolent swishing, round and round and back again.

"I was born during the War, World War II." He marked this specification with a slight forward bob of his upper body. "In a town that was heavily hit during the fighting when Germany at last was taken."

He continued. "Many families did not easily learn of the fate of people who fought for our country or where they might have died or been buried. My own father fought for Germany until his unit was captured by the U.S. in 1944. Most of them became American prisoners of war but we never knew that. The word did not reach us. My mother was told that he was missing from the last major battle and then later, that he was presumed to be dead."

He paused and said awkwardly, "My mother kept a picture of him on our wall, and I think still believed he would come up the stairs one day until her last breath. But he did not. She did not ever know for sure that he had died, never knew a grave to visit or a day to observe." Again, the forward bob punctuated his words. He had obeyed her and that was important to him. Or perhaps to this story.

"In May of this year my mother died. I had always lived with her and when she died, I went to a reunion of my father's fighting unit. I found the information for the gathering as I was sorting through her papers. This was to be the first ever reunion of surviving German soldiers of my father's unit. I was curious to know something about him and thought to find the people who might have last known him." Pieter Becker stopped for a moment. "And so I took the train and went to the reunion. There was a very long board with much information pinned to it about the soldiers who came and went." He said quietly, "This unit had many deaths." He sat still for a moment.

"And so I gave my father's name, Franz Becker, and I was taken by a volunteer to my part of the history of the unit and began to read about his time in the troops." He took a sip of his tea. "It was a curious day. A small man, very quick and always moving, came and grabbed my hand. He said he would help me look for the name I gave him. And he knew my father, in many places, he said. So I began to ask him about when my father died and he kept shaking his head.

"'No, he kept saying, no, he did not die there.' And I did not understand what he meant. Perhaps, I thought, my father had died somewhere else. But he did not mean that either."

We were listening intently now, trying to figure out what brought this man here.

"Who was this man?" Cameron asked.

"He was Willi Prang." Pieter Becker looked again at the pictures. "He was a sergeant in the German army. And he was the camp coordinator for the German prisoners of war here in America."

"America?" I asked. "I am not sure I follow."

"Yes, this unit that my father belonged to was captured and brought to America in 1944." He paused. "This Willi Prang and I were very confused with each other for a long while. At last I understood that he meant by my father not dying there that he meant he had not died, that they had come to America as prisoners of war together."

Pieter's words edged through my grief.

"He knew him during their time here. They were at more than one camp together; the last one was a Camp Penn in Massachusetts. But then, Willi Prang lost track of my father when they were all shipped to England at the end of the war." He stopped and told us, "All German soldiers stayed in England on their way home, some for almost two more years."

"Yes, well," I said. Pieter Becker held up his hand.

"And then Willi Prang was surprised to know that my father never came home."

"They didn't stay in touch?" I asked.

"No," Pieter Becker shook his head, "The war was such a big thing for these men, many of them at this reunion were seeing each other for the first time in all the years since. But that is not what we talked about."

He went on, "He said he happened upon my father when he was on a trip to New York City in 1975." He laid his hand flat on the table next to the third picture. "With this man." He pointed to Matthew's photo.

It sounded too odd to believe, "Are you sure?" I leaned forward to pull the image toward me. There was my father looking straight-on at the camera, no doubt.

Pieter Becker replied. "Willi Prang took this picture," he said. "And gave it to me himself. He said that he took two of them and that he gave the other one to my father and this man. They were together, he was sure, and that he did not know which one of them would have it. That he did not know where it would be now."

Silence fell. Cameron chewed ice as though he hadn't a care in the world and then asked: "How did you find us?"

"I read the notice of Matthew Rankin's recent medal in your *Stars and Stripes* magazine," he said. "I had just been to the reunion and found out about Franz Becker. I had gone to the library to research, to find out something. I did not know yet what I was looking for, just seeking information to start with."

"How did you come across Matthew's name?" I asked him. The picture from Stars and Stripes was one thing, but how had he gotten here?

"A ribbon that he wore in that *Stars and Stripes* issue, they put it in the caption of the picture.

"I could see from the face that it was the same man." He paused. "The librarian told me to contact the International Red Cross, that they give help to World War II survivors who are looking for family. I did and they sent me to an office that the

Armed Forces keeps. I had the name. And they found a Matthew Rankin who had won the ribbon for courageous service. And I had the picture."

He stopped speaking for a long minute. "Camp Penn was part of Kenneth Air Force Base." He said.

Kenneth had been Matthew's last active duty assignment from the Pentagon.

"I got a copy of that picture made. For three dollars. Then I began to ask around." He paused and looked at Cameron and me. "Old soldiers talk a lot. They sit and remember the details of each day, or a certain march, or the battle and minute that someone died. I thought that I could probably use that talking to find more out about my father. But I kept coming to nothing. So I decided to come here, to find out if the man in the picture could tell me more. They did a further search for me and found a picture of Matthew Rankin retiring from service. And the man in the pictures is the same. Different yes, from whatever the years in-between brought him, but the same man. And I decided to come and find him. To ask about this."

He paused again. "A lot of people, old American soldiers, visit Germany in these years. There are reminders everywhere of that war."

"There should be," I said.

"Yes, there are. Of all different kinds. Some are markers put up by groups and some are the buildings that the Third Reich used. And everywhere are burned and bombed hulls of buildings. It is not possible to not remember over there, the war that country fought."

I thought about it. We had studied it, a seemingly long ago time and place and event of history, when we were in school. But for kids, if something happened before they were born it was distant and unreal, not an everyday touching you flesh-and-blood thing.

And now? That a long-ago time of Movietone footage and old war movies was actually, possibly touching my life on a sunny morning in 1996.

I said, "But it was too late. Matthew was gone."

"Yes, I was already on my way here when he died, I think. Traveling, I did not know of the death. And when I got here you tell me he is gone. But I want to know, if I could, some people who knew him. I am very curious about these two men." He stopped and shrugged.

I sat back and sipped my tea, thinking that I knew the height and weight and favorite foods of my father, but not the inside of the man he really had been.

Pieter said, "Can you add to this story some details that might take me a little further to finding out what happened to my father?"

"I don't think I know anything, but I'll try," I said neutrally, not sure yet of what I wanted to commit to. "It has been a lot of years since I thought much about the time I lived on that Air Force Base."

Pieter nodded, relief in his face. "Just your willingness to look is appreciated," he said. "I know this is a hard time for you."

I thought that maybe Ginny was right, maybe staying busy was the best way to deal with the silence. Pieter gathered his papers into the well-creased envelope, all except the picture of the two men in what seemed to be Grand Central Station in New York. When his hand came to that it wavered and then pushed it slightly my way while looking at me with raised brows. Would I want it, the look asked? I nodded. He hesitated and beside me Cameron said; "That is the only picture you have of your father, Pieter?"

"No, it is just the only copy of this picture." He ran his thumb across the surface of the faded photo on the table. "It is just I have so few of them that each one is maybe a little bit more that I did not know."

"Then make a copy for us, and you might want to make one to use and put that one away somewhere safe." Cameron gestured at the shot. "We are just now hearing about all this, so we have enough to think about until you can bring us a copy."

Slow down, was the message in Cameron's words, *let this settle a bit*. His caution was a good thing, I had often found.

Pieter took that photo too, tucking it also into the envelope, saying he would find a place to make copies. Cameron saw him out, then came back into the room. The stillness held a beat, a throbbing, as we looked at each other.

"I wonder what Matthew was up to," Cameron said and slid into the rocking chair.

"Maybe nothing," I said. "Maybe it is just a picture of someone he met."

"Well, it is that, but there are not many pictures of you guys, are there?" Cameron asked.

"No." I had to agree. Matthew had never been one for taking or posing for pictures. If he did, in my memory it was a situation or a moment he felt needed it, or more likely one that he could not get out of. Of my childhood there is a single tumbled box of photos, including the naked baby pictures that no one ever wants discovered.

I rose and gathered the tea glasses to rinse in the sink. Beyond the kitchen window I could see the giant pecan with our bird feeder hanging from the stump where a giant branch had been cut off years ago. I glanced at the slant of sunlight.

Every day, about this time, a tiny squirrel ran down and paused on the sawn off stump and considered the bird feeder swaying lightly in the breeze. He ooched out to the farthest point of the stump and stretched down toward the bird feeder, tiny front legs reaching and grasping in the air, anchored to the tree by his back feet. Every day he tried and every day, or most of them, I watched him. He remained sure that one day his stretch would be enough to reach the seeds in the feeder. He was still hoping.

I finished the kitchen and decided to start a load of clothes, all the while thinking about the help Pieter had asked for.

I walked through the house with a laundry basket, gathering towels and tiny shorts. If you wash once a day at our house you have one load, if you wash every two days you have four. In each room I could see Matthew, which was natural, since this had been his house. Matthew in his recliner by the window, reading. Matthew walking his dog. Matthew at the door, saying goodbye to us as we corralled the girls into the car.

I switched the washer to hot, and water trickled in, steam rising against my face as I stretched above the open top for the soap on a high shelf. I waved a hand to move the dampness on and thought that the cloudiness was also in my mind. I could see Matthew in each of those places but could not remember the words or happenings that went with each moment.

Hours later, I still puzzled about it as I sighed and sipped my tea. The evening was close and still; the air had grown heavy with more rain to come. Above us, the ceiling fan hummed in lazy circles, stirring air that did not cool, and the papers on the table.

"Bed?" Cameron asked. It had been a long and exhausting day. I missed the girls, the sound of their nighttime silliness, yet I listened to the quiet with welcome too. I brushed my teeth and put on the old soft t-shirt I sleep in. As I turned back the sheets, the smell of fresh laundered cotton wafted up, and they were smooth and cool as I slipped between them. Cameron was already asleep on his side of the bed. I rolled to turn out the light and settled into my pillow, watching the dark lines of branches fall across our white curtains. I closed my eyes.

I dreamt then of a strange mist along the ground spread thick and soft as cotton batting. Somehow I knew this whiteness could only bear the weight of dreams, not even that, if they were heavy. Beneath the fragile mist, sadness gathered like the gray of rain unspent.

I rose and hovered for a moment, then began to move rapidly, skimming over the clouds.

Suddenly a figure loomed in front of me, boom, appearing so suddenly that I blinked and flinched, startled at the largeness. I knew I really didn't blink for I knew that I was dreaming. Did one blink in dreams? And if I did would I remember? The blinking? The dream? The dream-thinking that one does?

The figure turned a little more and I started, knowing the jaw line and long, tall height. It was a man in a baggy, bloused flight suit, a leather flight helmet dangling by the straps from his right hand. Who he was lay just beyond the pale of my mind, his features shadowed by a light from somewhere else.

Then the mist swirled in and the figure was gone and I waked to Cameron shaking me, saying, "Manda, it's a nightmare." I lay, breathing heavily, as if I had been too long under the surface of ash or sea or dream, oxygen deprived. I was giddy-nauseous from skimming over the clouds. As if I really had done so.

"What?" Cameron asked me. "What?"

I shook my head, I couldn't answer, didn't know. I threw back the sheets and swung my legs over the side of the bed and into the morning, frowning, eager to put the nighttime in its place.

At sunrise the images of night recede like tidelines left when the water's gone. But an edge is left, bits and pieces of what the nightswell held. That's how you know you were there, somewhere you need to remember before you can go on.

I sent Cameron on his way with a kiss and smile. I didn't tell him of the flier in my dream.

Chapter 4

July Days

In the days after the funeral, life seemed made out of cardboard. Colorful and detailed, to be sure, but thin and stiff. I drove on errands and did all the usual things. On a hot and windy afternoon, I picked up dry cleaning and stood with the plastic bag whipping against me and watched the busy corner beyond the parking lot.

The smells of Short Stop burgers and fries vied with the rich, spicy scent of the Oriental Garden across the street. Sweat trickled down my legs as the sun moved overhead, and to the north a dark line of thunderstorms rumbled into sight. Summer storms are not cooling in Texas. When the first raindrops fell, heavy and warm, I just stood and let them wash over me, the bag fluttering in my hand like a trapped thing, stuck now to my legs with the rain's wetness. The storm felt good, elemental and strong, a thing I could see and understand.

I wondered briefly where Ginny was, in a place of hot bright sun or cool and shadowed grayness? I tried to imagine, but could not see her in either setting.

The night before I had dreamt of Matthew on the stretcher, seen the second hand on the clock at the hospital, replayed in my mind his slow sinking to the ground, thinking of what more could I have done that might have saved him. I kept waking to wonder who lay in the coffin. It was not real to me that Matthew was gone.

With daylight these images receded, but I carried the niggle with me through all the moments of my day. I was unsettled with Pieter's coming and Ginny's going and my staying in one place. Grief and tiredness made me restless in the evenings, pacing and picking up and putting down things all around me until Cameron, exasperated at my unease, asked, "What can I do?"

"Nothing."

Cameron did not like things he could not fix. I am not one to let others fix for me. It is an ongoing tussle that we have. My raising commanded that you don't sit and wait for a hand squeeze; you get up and get on with it. But at that moment I did not know how or what to get on with.

In the meantime our cleaning frenzy continued, spreading now to include new paint and polishing the wooden floors. Until, that is, the air conditioning gave a giant sigh and one last wafting breath of coolness. Then silence.

"That silence doesn't sound good. Something isn't running." Cameron got up and went outside, and I heard the breaker box squeak open. This house, old and solidly built, came from a time before air conditioning. The inside unit sat in the narrow attic, and sometimes the strain of so much running in those hot and heavy days shut down the breakers.

But Cameron came back in, saying the breakers were fine. Then he looked at the ceiling. At this hour the attic would be stuffy and hot. But it was only going to get hotter. With a sigh, Cameron moved to the narrow attic door in the hall. I followed and watched him open the door with a squeal of swollen and long-stuck wood. A fine drift of dust floated around us in the air. Cameron peered into the opening. Narrow stairs ran up at a sharp angle into the dark above. He put one foot on the bottom step. The wood creaked loudly and he backed down in a hurry.

"No one's been up there in awhile," he said. "Did your parents ever use it?"

"No, there's only a narrow area that's usable," I said.

Cameron set foot again on the stair. Though the wood protested, he got to the top and disappeared from my sight. I heard the snap of his flashlight as he turned it on, and the beam played near the door for a moment before Cameron's footsteps moved away.

The quiet stretched out; then an hour later a rumble above me signaling that he had found and fixed the problem. I smiled a little and went on sorting books for giveaway. Another hour passed and I realized that Cameron was still up there. Curious, I went and called his name. Sitting in a dusty, close attic wasn't my idea of summer ease.

"Hey," his face appeared above me. "You should come up."

"It's dark and probably dirty," I answered. Dark and dirty are things I do not like.

"Yeah," he said. "You should. There's all sorts of stuff up here."

"Why? There can't be much," I said.

"A slide projector and a box of stuff," he answered. "Did your parents ever do slides?"

"No," I said, "We never had a projector, even back when all the families used them for trips. You know we didn't take many pictures."

Cameron nodded. "Hmm."

"Maybe it isn't theirs," I said. *Someone else had owned the house before Matthew and Ginny. Had they left it?*

"Perhaps," he said, "there's a chest up here with Matthew's name on it. The projector's next to that."

I went up the stairs then, curious. There couldn't be many photos to see. I wondered if, somewhere, Matthew was watching or listening, or whatever it was spirits do, saying, *oh yes, those old forgotten things at the top of the ladder.*

I stepped gingerly onto the thick planks and walked their length, moving carefully past the air conditioning compressor. As I passed beneath the single naked bulb, my shadow grew with each step until it lay stitched to my feet and stretched to where Cameron sat with his back to the limestone block chimney.

At last I reached him and slid down alongside him to look at the things spread out. An old blue footlocker with "Rankin" stenciled in white across its front lay tucked tight against the rough stone. Through the ventilation grills in the end wall, motes of light hit the floor in front of me, the pieces of dust and chaff I'd stirred up dancing in the beams.

I ran a finger along the hasp and lock on the front of the chest. Gray dirt came away, caked in a ridge on the end of my finger. No one had touched this in a long, long time. My finger left a mark along the dusty surface that shone a deep, true Air Force blue. Matthew's footlocker from his active duty days.

Small rustlings in the inkiness beyond my pool of light raised goosebumps on my arms. I had never liked sounds I could not find.

When I was a child, I was indelibly frightened on my first visit to the creek-bed below our house. That day, we descended into the cool half-light of thick grown cedars and passed into the shadow of the overhanging limestone cliff. As my eyes adjusted to the dimness, details became clear, the waft of leaves in sun, the reflections from the pooled creek. And something else. I looked closer. The cliff was pulsating. Up and down. Thousands of long-legged spiders standing on and near each other doing spider push-ups in unison.

They said I didn't quit screaming for an hour, would not hear that spiders were good, cried myself to sleep and wouldn't go under the cliff again until a very long time later.

"Cameron, let's take these down, okay?" I said and shuddered. I could feel eyes watching me, lots of them. He nodded, and we wrestled the chest along the edge of the floor and bumped it through the doorway and down one step at a time until we reached the hall floor. The projector was easier; it was in a bulky plastic case with a handle to grasp and latches on either side.

We pushed the chest and projector into the den and looked at them in the sunlight. Fine gray dirt covered all the surfaces except where our hands had left clear marks in the filth. Two tiny spiders did indeed dart away across the floor. I jumped, and Cameron shook his head.

Cameron took the projector case outside and wiped it down on the back porch. When he brought it in again, we set it up on the coffee table and opened the latches to lay the top back. These old cases had a built-in slide tray, and this one held a package of taped and wrapped dark plastic. Through it I could feel ridges like corrugated cardboard.

I got scissors from the kitchen drawer and cut open the end of some kind of oiled wrapping. When I laid it back, I could see "acid-free" printed on the inside. It was a tray full of tiny cardboard squares. Slides. I leaned forward and started to lift one out.

"Wait." Cameron got up and turned off the overhead light. "Old film can get really fragile, and someone packed these away well," he said. "If we want to see what is on these we need to work slow and careful."

He unwound the projector cord and ran it to the wall socket, flipping the switch. A fan began to hum and chatter noisily as the motor warmed up. "The bulb's probably burned out," he said. But a minute later it gave a flicker and then glowed steadily brighter until it reached full strength.

Cameron snapped the slide tray into place on the projector. He picked up the hand-device for changing slides and clicked it once. Twice. Each time bright, blank squares flashed onto the wall. On the third click, a fuzzy picture flashed onto the wall in front of us. Huge and distorted, it was hard to tell what the picture was. But in one corner a squat building stood next to a flat expanse of concrete. I looked closer. Negatives keep color and clarity so much better than prints, but these were black and white and details melded together into a monochromatic tone.

"Wonder what that is?" Cameron said.

Recognition blinked far back in my memory, and I knew where and what. I said, "It's the Air Force base I lived on years ago. That's the control tower at the runway."

Many, many years ago. When I had been sixteen. Cameron kept on moving through the slides.

Click.

There was Matthew sitting at a desk in front of two crossed flags, the official base commander. The picture on Ginny's bedroom wall.

Click.

There was Matthew, one foot resting on a jeep's running board in front of a fringe of pine branches. In the background a deeper gray was the bay meeting the lighter shade of the sky. An arm of sand curved away to the left, just visible in the branches.

Click.

There was Matthew in front of a small shingled house. Just standing, like people do when posing. It reminded me of the pictures you take of friends and relatives when the good times are all done. You aren't sure what to do with this person now, so you take a picture of them to mark the moment in between then and now. Here and gone. Past and present.

Click.

A screen of trees and a sandy incline with tumbled railroad ties heaped to one side. I started and Cameron glanced over at me.

It was another place from long ago. Tunnels. I had not seen them since a day in 1975 when I had ridden my mare to the far side of the base and found old tunnels laying abandoned in the firing area of the base. Tunnels I had promised not to talk about or visit again, or ever mention again. And now, here they were.

Click.

And then there was a slide of a shot very like one I had seen before. Just recently. Just yesterday in fact.

A shot of two men in a train station in front of the swirl of a crowd. This one was from a different angle, more from the side, and in the far background was a huge arch and the words Grand Central.

Grand Central Station in New York? Pieter Becker had said Willi Prang saw Matthew there. Both the men looked intense, eyes gazing straight at the camera with a heaviness of purpose you could almost feel. Studying it, I thought that they had allowed the picture because it would have been awkward not to. But they did not smile or appear to be enjoying themselves. Here was Willi Prang's other picture. Or a slide of it, anyway, which meant the picture had been in Matthew's keeping at some time.

I sat staring at the slide. At the two men together. I don't even know what I thought at first.

"This is weird," I said, and butterflies began in my stomach. How odd to have the same picture appear at my door just the day before. I took the clicker from Cameron and went through the whole tray again, seeing in them bits of buildings and stretches of road that I remembered. It was a long time ago, a time I had not thought of in ages. More than twenty years and two thousand miles away.

I pulled the chest over to the middle of the floor and opened it. Perhaps inside would be some explanation of the projector and the slides. Cameron watched me for a moment, then switched the projector off and joined me on the floor.

We sat cross-legged, knees touching, sifting through the entire box and thumbing through the journals and diaries of other times and places rubber-banded into neat, small bundles. But there was nothing that mentioned anything more than daily routines about the base. There were calendars and old notes and two broken bits of pencils, but there were no references to pictures found.

In a bottom corner a soft wad caught my eye. I reached in and, with a rush of pleasure, recognized a long silk scarf, crumpled and dirty. I lifted it out, delighted, remembering. Once the color of heavy cream, one end of the fabric was now almost black. The fringe tickled gently; the silk was old and richly woven and, even darkened and dust-laden, the material slid smoothly through my hand.

"What's that?"

"A flier's scarf," I answered. "It was Matthew's."

Cameron quirked his eyebrow at me. "Did Matthew fly?"

"Only for fun," I explained, "but he was given a leather helmet from World War II. This was with it, folded up inside one of the earflaps when it came. He always kept them together."

Cameron leaned over to peer inside the footlocker. "No helmet here now," he announced.

"No," I agreed and stroked the scarf some more. "I haven't seen it in a long time."

We sat for a moment and watched the aged silk in the light, golden now, for the sun had moved across to the front of the house, and the light was diffused as the afternoon settled in.

Soft light is kinder to memories. Maybe it is because we tend to cast remembering in a rosy glow so that all sharp edges fade away.

****

I dreamt of me. I was flying down a long hill on my blue ten-speed. On either side I could see my life as I whizzed by. The wheels spun so fast they looked like they were going backwards. At the top was my life now, the recent funeral and headstone peeking from just below the crest of the hill. As I headed for the bottom, my life unrolled in reverse.

At first I was so busy seeing my past that I didn't notice the sound. I was wearing the flier's scarf from the chest, and it fluttered and blew around me so that I also watched to see that it did not wrap into the wheels or spokes.

I heard a sputtering, slapping sound and at first I thought it was a playing card in my spokes. Then I thought it was the fast fanning of pages of a book, old and yellow and stiff, wet once and dried again to a rustling stiffness.

Then, as I coasted to the bottom, all the lights dimmed away except for a spotlit scene, and I realized that the sound was the flapping of a filmstrip.

Behind me a film projector whirred and clattered and I turned and found the sound.

In the spotlight sat a man on a stool, like a comedian on a stage. The man sat with a familiar posture, ramrod straight even while relaxing, though he was in silhouette just yet, shadowed by the light behind him. The lines fit a shape I knew. Matthew.

The figure stirred then and raised his head and said, "Manda."

I jumped. I had not heard his voice since the day he died.

"Yes," I answered. Part of me said, *you are dreaming*, but not a big enough part to stop me wanting to inch closer, to step into the edge of the spotlight's circle. *You are talking to a ghost*, my other self admonished, and my own self smiled back. *Silly self*, the smile said, *many talk to ghosts, but it only is the chosen to whom the ghosts talk back.*

"Why don't you come closer?" he said. Now he was wearing the flier's scarf, and I looked down to find I no longer had it draped around my neck. Though we had not touched, something had crossed over. My hand held the projector's control tightly.

"How much closer?" I asked.

Matthew smiled, "Just enough to talk, is what I had in mind, but it is within your control, you know."

I looked down at the control in my hand.

"The slide projector?" I asked. "The one from the attic?"

He nodded. "Yes."

"It has us curious," I said. "I don't remember us doing slides."

He cocked his head.

"We didn't."

The projector began to whir and rattle as though the fan was coming loose. Matthew glanced above my head at something, then his gaze came back. He pointed toward the slide button and said, "It is up to you, what you look for." There was a last flicker and he was gone.

I woke. Across the room Cameron was dressing, and I lay and watched as he slid into a t-shirt and jeans, zipping the fly as he crossed the room to check on me.

"Morning." He sat on the side of the bed and smoothed my hair. "How are you today?"

I frowned. "I had a weird dream," I said. "About Matthew. About this projector and the attic." The clearness of the man in the pool of light, so sharp against the dark, was growing wobbly and vague in the face of the morning sun.

A trace of rose scent came through the room on a breeze and birds chattered loudly. The white curtains drifted out from the window, and next to me Cameron smelled of good soap and toothpaste and sun-dried clothes. Real and light and fresh and a long way from ghosts.

"What about them?" Cameron asked me, rising to finish getting ready.

"I don't know, but I think I am supposed to look for something," I said.

"Well, we all have strange dreams at times." He finished stuffing things into his pockets. "With everything going on lately, I'm not surprised at you having them, though. The dreams, I mean."

He sat again on the bed and pulled me close for a hug.

"Going to call Pieter?" he asked against my hair.

"I thought about it. Though right now I don't really know anything except that I have a picture of the same two men in a slightly different shot."

I looped my arms around his neck and didn't let go, wanting his realness to keep me anchored. He sat for a minute, hugged me back and then pulled away. "Got a day to do," he said, and he was gone.

All day I kept thinking of how the picture of the two men was mixed in with a lot of other pictures of a place I used to live.

Was there a reason? Or did Matthew just keep all of his slides together?

I phoned Pieter Becker's hotel and left a message that indeed, a similar picture had turned up.

He phoned back almost at once, the voice soft, the accent smooth and heavy.

"May I see the other picture?"

They say that a picture is worth a thousand words, which is true, but you must know what words that picture portrays, which thousand words to sift for, listen to, remember.

Pieter and I studied all the slides, and the print he carried, bent and soft on the corner where he always held it. I noticed that he rarely put it down. But if suddenly I learned, at fifty-six, that I had a father and all I had was a few photos, I might hold them a lot, too. I was beginning to understand the drawbacks of a celluloid image when what you really wanted was the person.

In a black-and-white picture, eyes, even if blue, are only one more shade of gray. It gets hard to notice, to really see the fine small things that you might see if they were in living color. But asking of a memory is like that, too, black-and-white for the most part, and the color that we add is what we remember. Hindsight is different than the twenty-twenty vision of really being there.

****

"I wish Ginny were here to ask about this," I said to Cameron that evening when telling him of Pieter's visit.

"Do you?" he asked me. "Would you really call your mother and say, 'Matthew was such a colonel that I don't have a clue who he was.' Would you do that just after Matthew died?"

"No, I guess not. Not any more than I ever asked in all those years I could have."

"Actually, you couldn't have," Cameron pointed out with the logic I sometimes hated. "You didn't know what you didn't know until your father died. Maybe it's just coincidence that

Pieter Becker came along. Looking now has a direction because of things he has shown you that you don't know how to answer. Maybe you and Pieter are parts of some bigger puzzle."

I went through the slides again, clicking through the pictures. Frozen moments that might be just randomly placed together. And I was trying to make them fit in one last path to my father.

"There must be some answer somewhere." I said to Cameron.

He frowned. "But, Manda, the rest of the question is, does it matter much when you find it out? Each person has his own life, you know."

He kissed me gently and went to bed, leaving me on the porch to ponder why I was so curious, why I kept thinking that something was in the way of knowing the man my father had been. *Why is it that it's only when things are gone that we decide to miss them?*

****

Old soldiers talk a lot, ruminate and remember. I had grown up among such tellings and wondered now; could I find someone to ask about the little bits that I had?

Gil Hooper, I decided. If Matthew had said anything, it would probably be to Gil. Gil had taught him to fly small private planes, and later he and Matthew had served in Louisiana during the Cuban Missile Crisis.

Both of them always said that sleeping in the mud made you bond more with people than proper folks would approve of. He was as close a friend as Matthew kept in his last years.

I had known Gil all my life. Once our families had been close, sharing evenings of skiing and hotdogs at the lake as the sun went down. I called and asked to see him.

Austin sits on a fault line, the start of the limestone shelves and clear creeks to the west. East of town lies Prairie

Blackland, heavy black soil and tangled thick growths of small trees and vines. That is where Gil Hooper had gone to ground.

I bumped down a rutted road, small branches brushing the sides of my car. Halfway around the first bend I saw a flash of the old white house tucked back in the trees. Behind it stood the high old International that Gil had driven since I could remember.

"Manda." Gil stepped out onto his porch as I mounted the steps.

"Gil." I hugged him and kissed a cheek raspy with a two-day beard. The sweet dense smell of whisky clung close about him. Drinking was another lasting piece of many old service dogs.

"I miss him," I said into his shoulder, his old tee shirt and tears blurred my voice.

"I know, princess." His hand touched my hair.

He turned and led me toward two metal chairs turned toward each other on the porch.

"What can I do for you?" he asked me. One thing I liked about Gil was he didn't expect to visit where visiting didn't come. Just say it and be done. I thought that was what Matthew liked, as well, not wasting time when he did not have it.

On that late morning, I asked, "Do you know, did Matthew ever mention anything about German soldiers or World War II, or any prisoners of war?"

He sighed and rattled the ice in his glass. "Your dad didn't talk much about our serving, not like most of us. Why?"

I started to answer about Pieter, then didn't.

"Just poking around," I said.

Gil thought for a while. "His brother ran away, you know, at seventeen, and flew for the RAF. Flew bombers over Europe as a tail gunner, squished in that little bubble beneath the plane. Their mother almost had a nervous breakdown and Matthew, fifteen then, always hated that the war had taken him away. That his brother had chosen to go."

I pulled out my copy of the Grand Central shot then and said, casually, "Do you remember this man?"

Gill leaned forward and took it from me, holding it close to see the faces.

"Matthew, later on," he observed. "No, honey, he never mentioned anyone." He shook his head and handed the photo back. "Your dad knew a lot of people, with his job being so much travel. I don't know who the man is."

He stopped for a moment, then he went on. "I don't know, though, of anything since then about things German or having to do with prisoners. His brother didn't come home, but you know that already, I guess. Matthew served for a long time."

I thanked him and drove homeward. It was a bit more of my father than I had had before, but of a Matthew long before I knew him. Who was also not the one I was looking for.

If Matthew hadn't mentioned it, was it because it hadn't happened, or was it just a little thing? Or if Matthew never talked about it, did that make it oddly big?

I wondered again about the picture on the seat beside me. Who was that man with my father? Who was my father with that man?

Matthew's dark eyes gazed off the page straight at me, but still I didn't know.

Chapter 5

Looking

I came awake all at once with the urgent sense of missing something, of being tardy. The clock showed 7:00 a.m., later than I usually slept. I lay for a moment and listened to the day gathering outside. The house was long and dark and silent as I padded to the kitchen and felt for the light-switch, trailing my fingers along the wall. In our old house, I could put my hands and feet with sureness anywhere in any room, so often had I trod my paths. But here I was learning. My fingers found the switch and the room bloomed ahead of me. For a moment I found pleasure in the soft light shining off polished wood and stone floors.

The kitchen was at the far end of this long room, and its old wooden cabinets were mellow with age and oil, fitted with hand-blown glass panels of blue and white that looked like water running. I learned the wavery-ness of each pane as I set up my own kitchen here. Now I scooped coffee into the maker and breathed deep as the first strong smell of it spread through the room.

Thunder rumbled and dawn came as a heavy grey ceiling, dark and lowering. Inside, shadows lashed and quivered from branches tossed by the wind. It was the kind of day that seemed to absorb light.

I crossed the room and halted, looking closely at the corner by the fireplace. Did something flicker there, just beyond the pantry doorway? The very air seemed palpable, as though someone hovered there, just outside of visibility. As though the slide of light to shadow could bring them once more to being, and they might step out live in front of you, dressed and ready to chat.

I shivered, seeking something real to touch.

My gaze fell on our wedding picture, the moment of my stepping to Cameron and away from my father frozen in the shot. I took it up; it was through Cameron that I moved away from my childhood and into my own choices. On this dark morning the bright gladness of that day seemed even nearer, halcyon in memory. I do not recall the day for its trappings, but for what it brought to me.

Stillness. No motion, no current. The absolute absence of everything else. Sometimes I forget that stillness is not the same as emptiness.

Cameron's family sailed into Galveston Bay in 1847 and journeyed north in covered wagons through Indianola, which is no more, and San Antonio, until they settled at Sister Springs early in the next year. They claimed for themselves a limestone bottomed creek, with high cliffs and caves on one side and cypress, pecan and oak thick along the other bank.

Their family members included stonemasons and a teacher and several farmers. The house Bent and Doll lived in was built of hewn limestone blocks eighteen inches thick, and the floors are beams laid and notched into each other so tightly that no gaps exist even now, one hundred and fifty years later.

Cameron had run the same cliff top river trails so often that he no longer thought about where to put his feet. He just knew where the next good step was, beyond or before the twisted roots and crumbling ground. In the same pasture paths he had a lot of time for and to himself. I expect such ease comes from growing up with nothing around you that changes, so that the only change is your own.

I came to that place when we began dating, finding it a surprise. Service families moved a lot, ever the newcomers, and I had at last quit unpacking boxes on each arrival. Places stopped becoming home.

Cameron grew up on this land and loved it. I loved it, too, in the way that one loves something that you only know you wanted once you find it.

I met Cameron the night I graduated from high school, the official crowning of childhood. It was hot and still, a May night, so that the cold beer I drank did nicely to cool the sweat oozing from all over me, even at ten o'clock at night. I moved a bit to one side at the backyard party, knowing a lot of people, but none of them well.

That night a lanky boy in tight jeans was standing next to the table of drinks and snacks. My gaze skipped on and over him. Then the lanky boy turned and looked at the crowd over the top of his cup, among them and yet not of them.

My heart flexed a bit. Another observer, I thought. We rare ones tend to recognize each other. The difference was he belonged here, he had the ease, worn jeans and slouch that said he had been among these people more times than he could count.

Then his eyes met mine, and my heart did a funny flutter and settle, like a butterfly that isn't sure of the air, but knows it is time to fly.

Both of us eyed the other and then turned away for awhile, playing the mating minuet of "*I am not noticing you, I am not,*" and all the while having whatever side of you was nearest that person pull and tingle as though you were suddenly magnetized.

And the next thing I knew, I turned and he was standing right behind me, had threaded his way through the other sweaty people, and I never knew it. Never felt him coming.

Hmm, my heart said, *this one could be full of surprises*. By night's end his arm was loose around my waist, and so it has stayed.

At first, dating him was strange in the very stillness of it. Matthew's world had given me a lot of places, a range of experiences, but it held no gentleness. It was about gung-ho beliefs in guns and readiness and using them. A denial of feeling that Matthew made complete. At least the part of Matthew that I knew.

Our first Christmas together, Cameron roused me at 4:00 a.m. from my sleeping bag on the floor.

"Come on," he whispered and held out my sweatshirt. I followed him through a dark house until a door opened on noise and the smell of strong dark coffee, fresh donuts and a kitchen crowded tight with men readying for a morning hunt. An hour later we saw sunrise from an icy deer blind, shivering as the temperature dropped in a last bite before dawn.

Just at sunpeep over the ridge, an eagle screamed and the woods lit with dawn creeping through the trees. And Cameron's hand reached and twined tight with mine. He glanced at me and nodded to the morning with a slight smile that said, this is something I love best.

The next Christmas we hung a hundred small white lights in the crooked evergreen of Cameron's own new place and lay looking up through the boughs to guess which lights would blink on next. This time it wasn't a hill country dawn, but the smile was the same.

I cannot say when between those bookend days I came to know I loved him.

For how do you know when you love a person, the first time? How do you figure it out? Is it that your breath catches when you think of them? When you can't stop thinking about them? When your quiet moments are empty until you remember them again? For you never really forget them. They are so deep inside you that sometimes remembering seems extra. Startling.

You just are. The two of you. Together, all by yourselves. It takes stillness to find such ease.

In Cameron, I came to think of stillness like the mirrored surface of a pond so silvered by sunbeams that you must look through the reflection to see the secrets and treasures underneath.

A minnow darts from rock to frond, the surface rolls and settles, but doesn't break or splash as a wave might. It keeps within itself. You can see things in the water, if you only look.

Some people say they see other times in the surface, the future in the ripples. But, beneath the surface, sometimes it is only rocks, wet and colored, and sometimes it is more, brought by the river's music.

But what one hears as tuneful strikes discord in another. Cameron and Matthew learning to get along was like watching two people learn to waltz, and I was the music of their being. I expect it is like that for any two men who are so different from each other, so set within themselves.

Matthew thought the sun began its rise because it was 6:00 a.m., Cameron that 6:00 a.m. would happen, sun or not, and he'd take the day as it came. If dark, Cameron would find a flashlight, if light, he'd turn it off. Much more a person of the moment than Matthew could ever become.

The day that we got married, Matthew gave me away; he put my hand in Cameron's and looked him straight in the eyes. I stood between them and somehow a promise was made that did not wipe out my years of growing up. *Take care*, the look said to both of us. *Life takes some planning, believe it or not.*

****

I tried to think back to the self I was on that pictured day. It seemed to me that so many things in my life just happened, arising from circumstance. What if I had not gone to the party? What if? It was on those limestone river cliffs where I first hiked with Cameron that my own clarity began. It was there that I began to connect to something older than myself, as though the bits of arrowhead and pottery we sometimes found scattered in the dirt were talismans for me, signs that my walking where others had was something I was supposed to do. It was where I first realized that footsteps may follow each other, sometimes a hundred years apart.

"I feel like I've been here before," I said in my first visits to the ranch. Cameron's dad would quirk an eyebrow at me over his coffee cup as he upended it for the last swallow and headed out, saying the same as his son did and does, "Got a day to do."

But later I heard him saying to Doll, "She can't have been here before. The boy's just now beginning to date her."

Doll's soft response I didn't hear, but I told Cameron, "Your father thinks I'm silly." Cameron smiled, and it was all right. Cameron's father, a long user of this land, found only worth in its cattle and corn. But Cameron understood.

****

I broke my reverie and moved to open Matthew's chest, creaking the lid back until it rested against the tabletop. I reached and sifted through the oddments, in search of that ephemeral, elusive part of us we call the spirit, the soul, the self. Would any of them give me some bit of Matthew?

I brought the first rubber-banded group of small black books out onto my lap. They were a variety of calendar books, the pocket-sized ones that are so handy for jotting down things while you are moving about. Each one had dates and places noted on the first inside page in Matthew's angular hand.

I went through them like flip books and found a surprising number of details about my life noted on the pages. I fanned the pages, and my past went flashing by in a kaleidoscope of moments recalled from the cryptic notes on the page. "Manda-Montreal", about my trip to Canada. "Manda-birthday". "Manda-school". Through all the years, throughout his trips, Matthew had kept track of where I was. I hadn't known that, had always thought all home things were Ginny's forte. Which they were - a summary note is not the same thing as the logistics - but he had kept aware of the things I did.

I read through thirty-odd years of career and life, but I did not find notes of anything German. Trips and times and places were jotted down. Places he had gone often: New York, D.C., Boston, Texas, California.

New York? I looked again at the books, silent in my lap. He had not gone there in my childhood. Grand Central? It may have been my imagination, but the books seemed weightier than just moments before.

I was still there an hour later when Cameron found me. He was damp and smelling of soap, fresh from his shower.

"Morning," he said and sat next to me, reaching for me with one arm and my coffee with the other hand. I hugged him, feeling the familiar swells of rib and muscle under my hands. He was rangy and tightly drawn, and I felt a known thrill and hum at touching him.

"Okay?" he sipped my coffee and made a face. "Cold."

"I made it around five," I said mildly. "And I'm fine."

Our cat with the saucer-shaped eyes, Plato, joined us, rubbing against my ankles and then sitting between my feet to stare at the open chest on the tabletop. After a few minutes, he jumped up next to the chest and then dropped inside it to just sit and think about this new place.

We named him when, as a tiny kitten first come to us, he would sit and look at a toy, then up at us, as though to ask what we wanted. He had never played and would sit for hours watching something we could not see.

The usualness of Cameron and cats was a welcome touch in the dark morning and brought me back from my wanderings.

I thought back to Pieter's visit. He had gripped the most recently found photo tightly, his thumb squarely across Grand Central. "Three pictures now of my father, I have," he had said. "Many years apart." He bobbed his head, his excitement quiet and taut.

Now I thought of all the time I did have with Matthew, all that I had not learned. Regret poked sharply at me, remembering Pieter's pleasure at this other photo of his father. It was a little thing.

But a little more does not satisfy when a hunger is growing. It whets the appetite, brightens the dream, and the practical person begins to say *what if?* What about a little more? What if...I owned a gold mine? Climbed a mountain? Knew my father?

We began to imagine what once we did not dream might be, and now could not envision being without.

Pieter was no exception; he studied the picture and leaned forward to point at the partial words in the background. "Where is this Grand Central Station? Show me," he said.

And I did, on an old tattered atlas I dug from deep within a cupboard. He bent close over the page, fingers tracing the fine red lines of the map.

In a while a taxi carried Pieter away with one more image of his father firmly within his grasp. I had glimpsed a bit more of the man my visitor was. His eagerness to know reminded me of a child's wishing for Santa.

Cameron and I sat after dark, with our feet up and big glasses of *vin nobile*, an almost-black Italian wine on the table between us.

"I might," I said to Cameron, "want to look." I think I expected resistance, rational reasons why not, a reluctance to see this need.

"I think you should." Cameron nodded. My eyes filled with sudden tears, and he took my hand across the space between us. He said gently. "It's tough, this missing you're carrying for your dad."

I cried for real then, tears sliding as I sipped my wine. Not from grief, but with the sheer relief of admitting I needed to find something out.

****

Once I saw a movie in which a small plane carried someone to a place they had long wanted to go. To be. The tiny plane swooped down from a heavy fog, the kind where you are traveling, but the only thing outside the window is grayness pressing in. As you go lower in the plane, the clouds thin beyond your window and flashes of the land below began to appear between the cottony shreds of clouds that still flit by, as though reluctant to let go.

The land you seek stands out in remarkable detail as you lean toward the window, your heart thumping with the anticipation of being there. As you fly over, that is the moment of really getting home. Those on the ground will know you have arrived, will nod and go about their business, saying, *yes, she is coming, back where she belongs.*

And when you do arrive, everyone is glad to see you, but the rightness of your being back is so complete that no one makes a fuss. It is where you belong, as they all knew, and only you ever doubted, did not cotton on. You are your own reason for having been away. But you would not know that until you went, so the journey was not wasted.

I kept dreaming of the plane trip, of descending through the clouds, waking with a sense of hopefulness and homesickness for the place I knew I should be. I woke knowing what I had learned on the trip, but the middle step was missing. My plane never landed, and my home place remained a vivid but unreachable sight of red roofs bright against greenness, surrounded by the sea. Bright and clear and really there, but with no details and faces.

I understood that my little plane would not return to the clouds. There would be no going back. My journey was almost over, but where was I trying to go?

****

We first moved to an Air Force base when I was thirteen. It was like moving to another country for me, a civilian child. Matthew traveled a lot, and I knew he protected our country, but to a child gone is gone and here is here. Very black-and-white. We went to school in the winter and in summer we swam and played tennis, and later, bought and rode Skye.

Our mother said that in two hundred years we would not remember if the house was spotless, but we would recall a sunset swim or hotdogs on the grill, or sunrise as deer grazed, unaware of us watching from the cedar scree, stiff with morning chill. And those seemed to be the things that I remembered. I did not carry many memories of Matthew doing such things with us. Perhaps that was where our drifting began.

****

We Begin

And so suddenly Pieter was there with us in our lives. He came to dinner the next night bearing wine and light lemon cookies, and we began to know each other. There is a strange and sudden intimacy, a kinship within grief, in the absence of what has always been known, expected, existed. Vulnerabilities most often hidden, unsaid, become the medium for closeness.

My restlessness was that of loss, his of a sudden something in a place he had long thought of as empty, wound together with the puzzle of just what had he lost.

Before dinner, we sat talking of people we had known, of places. Looking for a starting point.

It must, we agreed, *it must be findable, seeable, mustn't it?*

He looked at the old rounder of slides and the projector and the prints heaped on the table.

"In science," he said slowly, "they start with what is known. One unknown thing at a time, that is the only way that you can know the effect of each new agent. Perhaps we should try that here. Start with what we know for absolute certain."

All our eyes swiveled to the pair of prints that lay on the top, of two men in a crowd of people. The only thing we had in common, our collective set, was that one small thing. A picture that held a man both of us knew, each somehow connected to the other. The then to the now, one shore to another. And to this minute when a man had come to sit in my living room and ask about a time and place I did not know.

"So much not knowing," I said at last, when the silence kept stretching out further and thinner. In my mind's eye, this tie was silken and small and strong, almost invisible, but a filament that bound us all, a weaving of events and people and times that brought us to this living room to sit and drink, wondering where to begin.

****

That night I dreamt that I sat on a beach overcast with the pearly light of a cloudy day. There were two of me, one watching the other. Out of the glare of the sun on the water came a man's figure, dark and slim hipped and solid. I already knew the bloused and baggy legs were those of a flight suit, tucked and gathered into the high black boots that pilots wore.

How did I know? one self asked the other. The other shrugged and went back to watching the flier. He walked until he stood over me. His head blocked the harsh glare of the sun and my eyes felt better. I could look up then at the halo lit figure above me.

I knew who he was well, without a word. He dropped to the sand, and I felt the thump where I also sat on the shore.

****

I woke then and went back into my life. Beside me Cameron breathed quietly. The dream receded, but the flier still waited on the beach just beyond the pale of my thought. He wanted me to remember. I could feel that; the message came back with me. I stretched under the covers and laid my hand on Cameron's back, putting this internal search aside for a while.

Later, I rose and put coffee on and showered while it brewed. I padded to the kitchen with comb tracks in my still wet hair, wrapped in a robe and poured my first cup.

The thing with remembering is that it is like casting a fishing net out to sink into the water and then pulling it up with a full catch inside.

Thinking back from now to then for most of us, is like laying the net open on the beach to see what we have found. There is more than one of many things, shells, but some attract our eye and others, our glance just slides right over.

We expect to see the proof of living right in front of us, whether it is cave paintings or a blockbuster movie or a telescope for the stars. *What else is there, where else must I look?*

****

The sky lightened then into a real feel of morning, and I decided to push the past back for a time.

I laid the notebooks back into the chest, first rubber-banding them back into their bundles. They had lain so long in these small groupings that the edges were folded in from the rubber bands and creases ran deep across their surfaces. One of the notebooks was bent, as though it rested long in the back pocket of a man who used it so hard that it bent to follow the curve of his haunch. Did he also carry a stub of pencil to mark it with? Or a tiny retractable pen?

I had learned one thing in this morning's musings, that gone is not gone. That Matthew in absence still had a sense of me. I learned that he probably missed me, a thing he never said. Regret ran sharp and icy again, and I was impatient with myself that I had not known that before.

I closed the lid then, and went out and got the newspaper. For once I would get to read it end to end without the jumble of questions that mornings brought from our girls.

I flipped the pages open to the Life section. I never start with the hard stuff. Morning takes easing into, and I do that with the more manageable difficulties of Dear Abby, the recipes I will not cook, and the trivia column that runs three days a week. Written by a local writer, the column covers everything from how to find items you have never heard of, to airing answers to a problem many people have shared. Sometimes it touches on the bits and pieces of history that bob, unbidden, on the tide of today's life.

Today the column ended with a brief note about the Texas Military History Museum. It suggested that you might pass on that unwanted Nazi helmet or flag. I had never heard of the museum. At the bottom was the name and phone number of the director to call if you had a question or something to give. Jack Harper.

The name was dimly familiar, and I sipped milky coffee and thought. Then I remembered. He too, had been a friend of Matthew's. I had known him once. My heart started to pound and I read it again. And ran down the hall to our bedroom.

"Wake up." I shook Cameron hard.

He rolled towards me and smiled, reaching for what Cameron likes best in the morning.

"No," I slapped his hand. "I know what the next step is. At least I think I know where to look," I amended.

He woke a little more and listened.

"You could be right," he said when I had finished, then rose to take his shower. Matthew had been stationed at Camp Mabry, home to this museum. It opened daily at 10:00 a.m., three hours and a lifetime away.

Chapter 6

On the western edge of Austin lies a historic cavalry post, Camp Mabry. Custer was here for a time, a short one, before his final trip to the Little Big Horn. Closer to our time, Matthew worked there before and after his Pentagon years.

I had known the place since my childhood. I dressed for the museum wondering if another visit would bring me further hints of the man who had been my father.

"Do you want to call?" asked Cameron. "Since you think you know this man who runs it?"

I thought and shook my head. "No," I answered. "Let's just go and see what it's like. If I'm wrong, I don't really want anyone to know it."

He didn't say anything else. It was only two miles from our house to the main gate. Today the short distance seemed miles more.

Mabry slumbered under giant oaks, amid a scattering of tanks and armored cars spread about the shadowed grass. Signs for the museum pointed past the old, sprawling trees to the huge double-doored building that had held the 149th Armored Division when I was a child.

Building 10, cavernous and dim, was once the stable, full of horses and hay and oats. On the inside brick were still the marks of old troughs and nails, rough and rusting even back then.

Matthew's first office that I could recall, from when I about four, had been here, along the west wall. I loved the building as a child and wondered now if the brick walls and heavy wooden beams soaked in smells I could just barely recognize. The ones I loved best, were even now so faintly scented they made me feel at home.

I could still remember the personal horses of the last general who had pastured them there. We had driven past their field every day when we picked Matthew up. I'd hung out the car window and watched them grazing in the late afternoon sunshine.

Now we walked inside, and a pert gray-blond woman rose from a desk by the door and greeted us. She took our money and offered us a brochure. The exhibit was laid out like a timeline, snaking through the battles and skirmishes of the years. The World War I display was highlighted this month. The war pieces lay in a lighted case, the most notable being the first aid kit displays just to the rear of two revolvers. The placing seemed ironic. Shoot, then bind the wound.

I asked after Jack Harper and she brightened. Knowing him brought her approval.

"He isn't here just now, but I will get you going. Where would you like to start?" Our guide moved her head back and forth with the small quick movements of a watching bird. "There is so much to choose from. The 36th mustered out of here in 1943," she went on brightly. "They trained at Camp Penn on the Eastern coast and then served in Italy."

The last of her words clunked home for me, like tumblers in a lock. Camp Penn was part of Kenneth Air Force Base, our home and Matthew's station in the 70s.

Things do come around, I thought. Had Matthew lain something to rest in a place that actually did have a tie to somewhere else connected to him? I squeezed Cameron's hand

and he pressed back. One step closer to my father. I felt it; this was where to look.

"World War II," I said right away, as though fascinated with her suggestion of the 36th.

"All right." She looked almost disappointed that we didn't share her difficulty with decision. But she didn't understand that I already knew. I just had to find out what it was that I knew.

When we reached the World War II section, our guide flipped a switch and lit the expanses of gray metal shelves stretching back into the dim corners. I walked the rows slowly. Some were filled and others mostly empty, an occasional dusty box squatting in the middle of an expanse of shelf.

****

They say, the veterans, that a war is different to each person that it touches. Stories have come of valor, courage, cowardice, evil, desperation and heartbreak.

But it's different when you see it in the dark aisles with nothing around but quiet, and odds and ends that soldiers brought home and tucked away. On both sides of us were carefully hoarded tools and talismans and totems, things that brought men home alive.

Only those who have witnessed the ultimate throwing away of life can understand the safeguarding of, the heartpeace found in waking to another day with a chosen oddment still beside you.

"For a lot of the guys, Manda," I suddenly remembered Gil commenting, "nothing before or after ever came up to that. The theatre of war was the most alive time; they felt it all the days of their lives. Those talismans brought them home, but they are also a bit of those moments. They make real again what hasn't been let go."

I walked slowly, Cameron behind me, closely reading the signs and labels affixed to objects and pages.

There were revolvers, helmets, crumpled pictures, a cross on a silver chain, dark with tarnish or blood or both.

I looked my question at the guide. *Where do we begin?*

"They are set up somewhat by battle theatre and time," she explained. "Space is kept for other contributions that might be from about the same time."

I nodded.

"Is it all right if we just look around?" I asked.

"Of course," she said. "Take your time."

She tapped away, her heels echoing across the cold concrete floor. Cameron glanced around again at all the shelves and said, "This is going to take some time."

We walked together through the tagged rows, through years of the war, until there right in front of us, high on a shelf was a section with a hand-lettered sign, *Memoirs and Diaries*. There was no time period.

"There." I pointed. Cameron moved to the section and stretched up toward the volumes.

"Which one?" he asked me.

"That one, the black one." I told him. "The one that says Rankin on the spine."

"Rankin," he repeated and looked from me to the book his fingers had closed around and were already bringing down.

In the eternity it took him to do so, I thought how lucky it was that we could touch these in the museum's infancy.

Then I had it in my hands, a black journal with a soft, stuffed cover and corners bent down and chewed by the years. With trembling fingers, I opened it to the first page and saw Matthew's spiky scrawl all across the page, tight and angular and definite, just like he had been. A second journal, a green one, was folded within it, too. I put that one to the side, looking only at Matthew's writing.

"Manda," it said, not *To Manda*, or *For Manda*. Not anything to make it a presentiment of what it was. Just *Manda*, almost as if it were doodled, faintly written in the margin. And I knew I was seeing what Matthew had left for me to find. I held it out for Cameron to see, and as he read the words I saw any doubt disappear from his eyes.

"I'll be," said Cameron.

A sudden wash of tears blurred my vision.

I cradled the plump volume in my arms and watched the dust swirl crazily in the beam from the high small window. It slanted past me to an ugly sofa, rusty brown and sagging.

"Why don't you go sit down," Cameron said, pointing toward the couch. "I'll be right over here." He moved to the next aisle, bending close to read something on a card.

Seeing the handwriting of someone just recently dead brings a shiver, like getting a message from beyond. I read the first word and began to learn something about my father.

The pages were written close and tight, and I worked at deciphering the squiggles that ended some of the longer words and paragraphs. Either impatience or weariness had mussed his writing until the words were more loops and flat places than actual letters on a page. But then, Matthew's gift had been action and decision, not the graceful, timed, patient words of people less driven than himself.

I would need time to do this, I knew, and got ready to close the cover when my finger felt a bulge along the bottom of the back inside cover. It was smaller than the pocket flap, and I slid two fingers in and eased a small booklet from the corner where it had been lodged. The same stained and yellowed color as the journal's inside, I almost hadn't seen it. I put it in my lap and leafed open the old, limp cover to read he first pages of my find. *Soldbuch* was stamped across the top in heavy black letters. Below it, a paragraph I couldn't read. The words looked German. I turned the page to the centerfold and held the book closer to the light.

Looking back at me was the face of the man in the picture with Matthew. A younger face, much younger, only this time in a German uniform with a German name. Franz Becker. I felt the air go out of me and the room spun, faint light and shadows growing closer to each other. I sank back into the mudbrown cushions, and that is where Cameron found me, hands on the book in my lap, shaking just a little.

****

Now knowing the museum director became a card in my hand. I asked for and got special permission to take home the handwritten journal. To the outside world it looked like a downtime diary, but I felt there must be something that made Matthew put it where it had to be found.

"That's fine," Jack Harper nodded. He had come in while we were looking. "After all, it's just been sitting in a box here all along. Probably won't matter to anyone else, anyway. You know how old soldiers talk. We've got a storehouse full of that."

I smiled and said thank you and left it there. He did not know that the words in my hand were as close to a clue to knowing his father as Pieter Becker might ever come. But I did, and we went home to call Pieter and find out together about the men we did not know, both of us searching for our fathers.

Chapter 7

In 1973, when I was thirteen, we moved to Cape Cod because Matthew had been appointed base commander of Kenneth Air Force Base. Only a handful of reservists ever filled that role in peacetime, when the active duty men were available. But the Pentagon summoned and he answered and came to Kenneth, built on the Eastern seaboard in the '30s.

In its heyday during World War II, the base had been a place of 90,000 troops and much bustle. Through the '60s it was kept on alert with the threat of the Cold War. When we arrived, that was years in the past. The troops were dispersed and the once busy base much silenced.

Kenneth still sprawled across 22,000 acres of the upper Cape. I never did understand the idea that to go down-cape is to the far end, to the point where Provincetown narrows into the sea, away from the mainland. But you do not argue with New England customs; many of them have been followed longer there than Texas has been settled. So we moved into a house on a base full of closed and boarded-up buildings, cut-down services and eerie silence.

I don't know which caused what, the empty buildings or my imagination, but a sense of being watched accompanied me most of my time there. Most days, I rode my bike to the barn after school, pedaling with a bridle on my handlebars through street after street of houses with blank-eyed windows and cellar doors that always seemed to come unlocked and bang open as I passed.

I rode with the hair on the back of my neck raised and stiff, a warning of some sort to myself. By the time I got to the barn, I would be out of breath and warm even on the coldest day, from speeding through the streets faster than the gremlins I thought might reach out and grab me.

At the barn there might or might not be people, but there was always a sense of the present, and my anxiety would subside. A radio would be left softly playing, and the horses would be running in the pastures.

At the sight of anyone in the evenings, they would crowd to the gates, ready to be fed. Even if they weren't yours, they thought that today you might not remember that and would accidentally let them into their stalls and fill their buckets with oats.

I would catch and bridle my mare, Skye, warming the bit in my hands so that the metal would lose its chill before slipping it into her mouth.

I loved best riding on the beach, even on chill, gray days when a coming storm pushed the waves high onto the shore. For a child from Texas, the expanse of sand and water and green was like a dream.

At home we had space, but here the ocean and sand along the water's edge packed to a damp consistency perfect for cantering, weaving in and out of the wavelets, watching the fishing boats come in at night. Skye reveled in the water, meeting every beach trip with an eagerness that matched my own.

I found friends hard to make in the world of tough and ready children that the services breed, and harder still to make them in the prim and proper small towns that lay outside the three gates to the base. So I filled my time riding.

Except in summer, evening comes early in the north, and the beach wasn't always possible in a place where darkness was full at four in the afternoon. I was used to the longer days of home.

I began to ride Skye in the sand arena at the barn. She always moved as if on her toes, as if she would leap into the air if only she knew how, taking her time in coming down. We started to learn dressage, working with a retired army captain who lived near the base. Disciplined and rigorous and needing lots of patience - for a while it took my fancy, and Skye excelled in the art of minute accomplishments.

Matthew took to coming by the barn in the evenings straight from work. I think he thought I did not see him. He would park behind the screen of stunted pines that edged the arena and watch as I finished working Skye in the fading light. As I slid down and walked her to the barn, he would trail slowly past us in his jeep and meet us at the big double doors, already swinging them open by the time we came up the road.

I had taken on feeding for several families with horses in the barn when they had a game or a commitment that kept them from the night stable rounds. I was there, anyway, I said, and would feed theirs as well as my own.

Matthew fell into helping me with the simple routine of feed and hay and clean water buckets. We went back to a place that held no treacherous places to fall through when the thin ice of conversation gave way and skating became floundering. He searched for things, I think, to ask me about.

He had missed so much of my childhood. And I did not do well with his orders to come here, to this Air Force base so far from my life up to then. For a while it was the only thing we had in common, this horse.

I think he liked the exactness of the rules and procedures of dressage. After all, war has rules and Matthew knew rules. He read up on the history of dressage, though he never mentioned it.

I would see him reading late in his chair in a pool of light, glimpsing the title as I passed by, silent in the hall.

I think now he was trying to find a way to reach me, a path through the rocky ground between us. I liked the little bit of time I had with him, perhaps wanted it, though I would never have admitted so. That would have been a weakness.

So I don't know if I picked dressage because Matthew watched it, or if he watched it because I picked it.

Skye and I had a flash of winning at the local level and briefly I thought of other competitions. Matthew planned out a schedule for us, a list of practice times and drills. But higher means harder and I did not want that. Instead of hours in the ring working with a coach, I wanted to ride on the beach and let Skye swim in the sea.

Matthew pushed harder for me to show, and in reaction I went further away, down through the pines and seagrass and sand trails. I knew no boundaries of time or fence. The more he wanted to define me, to set me within a frame, the more I wanted out of it, to be where and what he would not know.

Sixteen is a hard age at best, in any place, a time when you are just beginning to know what you want for yourself. A time when you don't want other people to want things for you. I shied away from his questions, his needs.

On a blowy afternoon, the sky so deep a blue that it looked in painted layers and white clouds moved by overhead like shreds of cotton, I biked to the barn and saddled Skye, eager to ride in the riffles of waves that touched the beach of the bay.

I checked my watch; it was already two and the sun went down at five. The only way I would make the beach that day would be to ride straight across the base. That area was off limits. It was a Tuesday, a quiet day, and Matthew made his rounds at two, so by the time I was where I shouldn't be, he would be back at his desk, making plans for the weekend drill ahead. My timing probably could not have been better.

I swung up and we headed out, Skye's springy walk and nodding head pointing to an afternoon of simple pleasure.

We rode out the gate to the barn and I aimed Skye through the fattest part of the base, wanting to get to the bay. I breathed deep, willing to me the pungent scents of salt and sun and pine. Sometimes that smell was awful, when something had washed up or died on the shore and the sun had not yet done its work.

As we moved among the pines the wind was almost stilled, just a breath that carried the tang of salt and the heavy smell of things drying on the rocks. Both sides of the Cape are ocean, one is open and tumbled by the sea. The other, the bay, lies within the curved finger, cupped from the east and north winds that can destroy in a moment houses and homes and lives.

I rode through sections of the base I did not know well, streets and streets of boarded-up, empty buildings, then a stretch of woods I took to be the edge of the base.

I rode up a small incline and tried to get my bearings by finding a fixture that I knew. I scanned the edge of what I could see, and back to my left I could see the long white sprawl of the closed base hospital within the trees. A wooden building set up on pilings, it ran long and narrow amid rails and ramps and stairs.

Ginny volunteered in the clinic that still crouched at one end, the only medical care on the base.

Once I had ridden up there and come across a small cemetery lying choked with weeds behind the last wing. I asked Matthew about it, and he found out it was where the command dogs were buried, a small place of honor.

I never rode there without a feeling of unease, a sense of someone about to tap me on the shoulder. And after they closed the clinic, I never went there at all.

That end of the base was far from any other activity and the emptiness wasn't empty, it was lonely and forlorn and spooky. I remembered that and shivered at sight of the small dark copse of trees with its flash of chain-link fence.

That day I realized that if the hospital was already to my rear, then I had come a long way. The beach shouldn't be much further. I urged Skye forward and she picked her way, easy and willing.

We rode for a long time before I looked at my watch. We should have found the Sandwich Road by now. In those days, that gate was closed and base visitors had to drive six miles to the south around to the Falmouth entrance.

But we had not crossed anything I recognized; the trees had grown thin and short around me, so that we were riding on open ground with more dead tree stumps than with fresh and living pines. I stopped Skye and stood up in my stirrups to look for a sign of a trail or a road or a fence. To my left lay something dark and solid. I moved toward it, and a jumble of old railroad ties and a pile of dirty bricks took shape. Beyond them yawned a dark hole, a doorway built at an angle into the ground. I halted Skye and slid down. Quiet folded around us; there was no hint of water or wind or cars or boats coming into harbor, a sound that should come up as we neared the bay. Just me in this place I had never been and I was lost, to boot. I moved forward and looked into the hole. Shallow steps ran down into a small, square area that led into a linteled doorway built into the rise of ground in front of me. I thought briefly of dugouts, pioneer prairie homes. But this was bigger. I stooped and peered into the dark ahead.

The tunnel went straight ahead, letting in slanting sunlight along its length until the angle of the doorframe cut off the rays. Ahead of me, I could see openings to the left and right. In the area just past the entrance several old barrels sat in a puddle against a wall. Then, from the dark, came a low-pitched growl and the answering snarl of a second animal beyond where I could see.

Wild dogs had been reported on the base, and I knew now why they couldn't be found. I had never heard the tunnels mentioned. But right then my focus was getting out of there before Skye and I were attacked. I scrambled up the steps and ran for her, my fingers fumbling to untie my reins from their knot around a flimsy branch. I swung up and kicked her to a canter and stayed there, a thing I never do, running her over new ground. Branches slapped my face, and she wove from side to side, finding the best footing on a trail she did not know.

I rode hunched close to her neck and let her pick her way. My neck prickled, feeling for all the world as though a hand might touch my shoulder at any minute, and a voice whisper in my ear. *What are you doing here, Manda? What do you want to find?*

I was almost crying, tears and wind and fear keeping me from knowing.

At last we burst from the trees on a narrow stretch of beach bound at each end by rocks and seaweed and almost on top of a startled duck. We were a long way from where I thought we would be. Around us was Falmouth's edge, settled, full of cottages lit with evening light and seaviews and horses in paddocks - normal, everyday things that made my fright a silly, imagined thing. I found a payphone on the corner of a dimly lit beach edge street and called for someone to come and get us. When the truck and trailer arrived, Skye clambered in, still spooked, as though the hiss and whoosh of the ocean in the dark was instead the breath of an unknown and dangerous thing.

All I said to anyone was we got overcome by the night.

****

Now I would think again about those years when we gathered to read Matthew's journal. This time Pieter brought two bottles of wine. A *Gewürztraminer*, light and sweet with the heat of the late summer harvest. *Spatlese*, they call it. He poured it into three carefully even portions and moved two of them toward Cameron and me. It winked rich and golden in the glasses and we each sipped and sat, ready to begin our delving.

On the table before us lay gathered our smattering of curiosities: the two Polaroid shots of a pair of men in Grand Central Station, an old unit photo, a soldier's I.D. book, a slide of stunted trees and old things heaped about in front of a dark oblong entrance to a tunnel.

And the journal.

I sipped again to wet my dry throat and reached to open the cover. My breath caught under my ribs and for a moment the words would not come.

Matthew's handwriting was tiny and crabbed but oh-so-clear. He told me years before that such writing came from taking reconnaissance notes in a tiny notebook lain across his knees in the cramped cockpit of a fighter jet.

The writing seemed to leap off of the paper, the spiky black words set in close lines filling each page.

Just the sight of the handwriting startled me, or perhaps it was the freshness of the ink on paper, crisp and dark against white, which was neither yellowed nor bent. As though it had not been much opened. That was how I could see Matthew writing it, looking it over once and then putting it away. Filed, mission completed.

I lowered my eyes and read aloud. My voice, cracked and high, filled the dark spaces and then gained in strength and cadence as the images spun out.

Chapter 8

Matthew, June 1996

What prompted the move was a murmur, not unexpected with Matthew's family history of heart attacks. But it didn't start with the blood. No, the murmurs began as much in his ears as in his veins. The new condo was spacious and sunlit, with no hubbub of its own. And in this silence Matthew finally heard a faint incessant chatter, sibilant whisperings that could not quite be made out. *Time is near.*

Time. The one thing you cannot change.

He woke tired now, a thing he had not done before. And he knew this last slowing would be the final one, because no amount of resting lessened the weariness. His doctor would not name this fey sense of what was to come, saying only that some things cannot be explained. But Matthew knew.

For a while he railed against this fate, becoming difficult and short-tempered. Matthew had not been a man to allow outside forces to chart his course. This time, beyond making a will and choosing a gravesite green and restful, he became aware of the people and things that would go on without him. Seasons and holidays and children and life.

So he set his house in order, putting things into place as though his thoughts and wishes and written words might keep these things always on the path he had chosen for them. They wouldn't forever remain so, but it pleased him to think he left tucked together items that made more of a difference than when these things were apart.

What he had come to think was that some things lie deeper than the surface of the life he had lived, that these threads connect with things months and years apart. That history repeats itself, that life is a cycle. What we do someday will touch those who come behind us. That time tracks back across itself in this world. It must, for there is only so much space. Now Matthew believed that more than anything else.

In his own fading, Matthew remembered the cornered things still in his other house, now Manda's. In the dimness of a closed-up space was one bit of string that he was not wont to throw away.

He chose a day when Ginny, his wife, was out with friends and couldn't say no to his driving. On that morning he made his way to Manda's house to find something he'd left in the dark upstairs, something that now needed to be found.

Even driving slowly was wearing, and when he pulled into the driveway he sat for a moment and rested. He loved this house under the heavy weight of green pecans that pulled the branches down close around the roof. Home, still, to his heart. It was an old house, almost one hundred years, built when this land had been beyond the edge of town. He was glad Manda and Cameron had bought it, would go on within its walls.

On the creek bank at the back of the lot he had once found a bit of an arrowhead stuck in the gray clay of the bank. And up the hill on the creek's far side lay the old Davis cemetery with graves from the 1860s. He had never been there, only recently learning that one of the original family's members, a neighbor, still kept the grounds. Finally, he stopped his rambling thoughts; inside was his mission for today.

He let himself in with his key and watched the amber window throw colored patterns across the tile as the door swung open. How often he had seen that? he wondered. How often had he looked across it and not noticed? His heart clutched and he could not say if it was from weariness or regret.

In the middle hallway, he opened an inset door to the narrow stairs that ran up to the small attic above. The short flight seemed monumental, and resolutely he took a breath and put his foot on the lowest step. One at a time, all other things grayed away until the next step was the only thing in his mind.

His heartbeat rose and thumped wildly in his chest and for some moments he swayed and gulped, willing the gallop to slow. One step at a time, he reached the top. When it eased enough, he pulled the string for the bare bulb that bloomed into dim yellow light.

He leaned for a moment on a stud that framed the opening and surveyed this long, narrow space in front of him. The peaked area was dark and dusty, tucked full of odd, old items that lay in a gumbo of uselessness. The wooden floor stretched away from him to the far wall of tongue-and-groove oak wood and the limestone blocks of the chimney. Boxes with frayed edges of things peeping from them lay sprawled across the space. The light did not reach much beyond the nearest edge of the jumble, casting deep valleys of shadow from one pile to another.

Against the endwall, an old cracked mirror leaned and gave him back two of himself, a silhouette backlit by the harsh amber glare of a naked bulb. The top right corner of the glass was cracked and canted so that a smaller image of him floated above the shoulder of the big reflection, a bit like a guardian angel. After a moment, his eyes adjusted to the dimness, and Matthew looked at his own reflection; a paunchy, grayed man in khaki pants and white tennis shoes who might walk his miles in the mall where people would glance right past with no inkling of the man he had been.

He sighed, and the image gusted away. He scanned the dim space beyond the boxes, anxious to know that what he sought was still where he had left it, between an old box fan and the sharp drop of the eaves. Yes, a dark, square shape still huddled tight against the chimney's side.

He picked his way through the boxes until he was next to the chimney and could grip its rough mortared surface in his fingers as he pulled the fan aside and lowered himself to the floor. His breath sounded loud in the closed space and once again he said to himself, *not a question of if, only of when.*

Cobwebs and dust layered the chest in a thick gray film. He put out a hand, then wavered, pulling it away. His touch would leave a track and a track is what, so far, he had avoided. By themselves, the items were just mementos, detritus, leftovers from a career served and completed. When the chest was laid away up here, things unsaid had been easier to keep.

Perhaps, he decided, it was better not to touch again things so long in his past. He closed his eyes and saw what he had placed there, a leather helmet with a long scarf rolled and tucked inside, a litter of small, soft-covered date-books, some military identification papers, two boxes of slides and an old projector in a plastic case with the cord wound close.

And a diary.

He wavered, then his hand came down and his fingers left clear blue spots in the dust as he fumbled for the latch. Laying the lid back, he reached inside and took up an old, black book. Another life lay in the pages. He leafed through them and wondered about simply burning them all in the rock fireplace while he was still alone. But July would be next week, and people would wonder at a fire in summer. And what the pages told was important.

Pretty soon now it would be too late for him to be the one to tell the story. For a long time he had held his silence, seeing it as his duty to his country. He had been raised to believe that loyalty included silence. The Air Force kept a smiling face turned outward and solved its own problems within. He had believed that, adhered firmly to it; until later.

The problem was that once, just once, a schism had appeared in the façade of duty, enough that through the years he had never cleaned out the footlocker, never thrown the items away. In the years since Cape Cod, since retirement, he had come to think that this story was not just his.

He had found it, certainly. No one could argue that point. But the story really belonged to the others in it, as well as himself. So his own silence would not break, but the telling he would leave, in case anyone did come looking.

And he knew who would search, whose curiosity almost became waywardness, who never had much to do with rules, but rather followed her own sense of rightness. Peculiar and strong as he'd found its direction, it matched his own in being a sense of purpose.

He looked at his watch, oh-one-hundred hours. His small chore had taken up more than three hours. Manda would be home soon with the little ones. He would go down and just let it seem that he had only stopped by for a visit. He took the diary out. Slowly, he made his way down the stairs and gently shut the narrow door, leaving the attic in darkness.

When Manda's key rattled in the lock, he was sitting in a heavy recliner, as though that was as far as he had gone. Linnea and Leah burst in, both talking at once about school.

"Guess what I did today, Papa?" Each voice was louder than the other, wanting to be the first to tell. Now he was content to listen, eager to gather the moments of which there would only be so many more. His heart clutched again, and he smiled at his daughter, and swallowed hard to keep the prickle of tears from his eyes.

Time is near.

Chapter 9

Matthew on Cape Cod, Summer 1973

H is transfer came through quickly, and Matthew spent the summer at Kenneth on remote assignment. His wife, Ginny, and children, Manda and Sam, joined him when New England's fall began. The cool greenness, blue ponds and coast cottages reminded him much of his boyhood on Long Island, with summers spent upstate.

"We're getting close," Matthew announced as they crossed one of Cape Cod's two bridges to the mainland. Next to him, blond and slender, Ginny watched easily; in the back, the two children stirred. Around them was the last flush of tourists going off-Cape and the drifts of fall leaves blowing and skittering in as though to take their place.

He lowered the car windows, and a breeze laden with salt and pine flowed into the car. He loved the scent and wanted them to, also.

The rearview mirror showed Manda and Sam watching pensively. Born in Texas, everywhere else felt and smelled strange to them. He felt impatience surge, and bit back a comment that lots of families move many times. At last they swung up to the main gate of the base with flags of country and state and units restless in the breeze. A uniformed guard stepped out of the sentry hut and held up his hand. Matthew rolled to a stop.

"What's this?" asked Manda from the backseat.

"Cool, guns." Sam was entranced and sat forward to see better, resting his arms on the back of Matthew's seat.

"You've got to be waved onto the base," Matthew answered. He met her sleep-flushed and questioning gaze in the mirror.

"Every time? But you run the base," she protested. The guard snapped a salute, and they at last drove onto the base, a small city-state that hummed and clicked through its days behind the guards and fences and screens of trees. A world within itself. His world. He felt contentment, glad to be back.

It would be a different world for all of them, used as they were to the heat and southwestern ways of home, where people said "hi" and food was barbequed even in the swelter of a summer's day. Here it would be different.

Matthew expected them to adapt to the comings and goings of his career. He was an officer and life fitted itself around that. It always had in his years of travel and long hours. But this was the family's first move to follow him to a posting.

His summer's stay had turned up a base stable, an officer's perk, and in the flush of money and the high-arc of his career, he shipped Manda's mare from Texas. She was there now, waiting for Manda at the barn. Surely that would please his daughter, and maybe bridge this distance between them that had grown so this last year.

Ginny accepted the idea of a move easily, serene in the idea of becoming the base commander's wife. Sam just seemed ready to melt into wherever they were, like the chocolate he was finishing now. Manda was the changeling, gone away into herself.

"There's lots of room to ride here," Matthew told her now, to say something into the quiet. "It's 22,000 acres, left over from the heightened activity of World War II. Some parts you can't ride on, but lots of it you can."

Manda nodded and asked could they stop by the barn, and Matthew thought no more about it.

Thirteen is perhaps always a difficult age, made more so when a mostly-absent parent changes the rules and place of a life. And most of all when the absent parent does not notice that all is not well for everyone.

In a military family, sympathy often remains packed away, boxed and in the basement of a family housing unit. Matthew reported back to work from his week's leave to relocate his family and expected that adjustment would occur.

He planned to make his morning drive to work as the sun rose and just peeked over the trees. Firm hand on the wheel, he sipped strong black coffee and crossed from base housing to headquarters where his office lay. At that early hour, the exact rows of buildings with buzzed grass and white-rocked edgings made him feel the master looking over his domain. Calm and neat and clipped, ready for action at any moment.

Matthew worked at home some on weekends, to be nearer his family. Despite his pre-occupation with work, he had watched Manda and Skye have a good reunion. She saw that the barn was nice, that Skye was getting used to a stall. But then the more Manda rode, the further she got from Matthew, the very opposite of his wishes.

Months after their arrival, he was reminded of that as he watched her from his seat on the second floor patio as she came in through the kitchen door, jeans and tennis shoes streaked brown with sand and salt. She was tall, dark and slender, and he felt more every day he spent with her that he knew her less than the one before. Her dark brown eyes held a depth now he never felt he plumbed.

"Been riding?" Matthew asked her, part guess and part just something to say. It was where she spent all her free time these days, often bicycling to the barn if he or Ginny were not home to drive her. Sometimes it was the only time he saw her in daylight hours, a small figure pedaling through the late afternoon sun while he was making a random round with one of the base police.

"Yep, I took Skye to the beach." Manda went inside and came back holding a Coke.

She opened it and took a drink, watching him read his files. Matthew shuffled a pile together and put it into his briefcase. He knew she hated that parts of what he did were something she couldn't see. But those were the rules of his job, classified and for no other eyes.

To Matthew, rules were a solid, known thing. He much preferred them to the vagaries of emotion and the reactions she constantly surprised him with. His own life at sixteen had not had much easiness. He had dropped out of school and gone to work. Manda should appreciate and enjoy what he gave her, but questions were not welcome.

"I didn't go right to the beach today," she told him. "I rode around some first."

"Mm-hm," he pulled across to him the sheaf of papers that had been delivered that morning, motor pool schedules for the coming week.

"I found something pretty strange that night you picked us up in Falmouth, and I want to ask you about it." She came and stood right in front of him, closer than she had been in awhile. He sighed sharply, and put the papers on the table.

"What did you find?" he asked.

"Tunnels," she said.

"Tunnels?"

"Yep, on the firing range," she said and tilted her Coke up to get the last swallow out of the can.

Matthew felt the warm sweep of irritation as he asked her, "What were you doing on the firing range?"

"Riding." She raised her eyebrows at having to give him that answer. "If you cut across it, there's an old road on the backside that nobody uses."

He watched her. "And there are tunnels there?"

"Yep."

"Don't say 'yep'," he corrected her. "It isn't ladylike."

"Well, anyway, there are tunnels there. We were riding and I went past some scrub pine toward a little hill. Skye stumbled and I got off to check her leg. All of a sudden we were in kind of a piled-up area of rock.

"It was weird because most of that part of the Cape is sand, not many rocks. I got off and started working our way through them, sort of picking a trail. I wasn't sure where we were, and I didn't want her to throw a shoe way out there."

Matthew watched her. She had his full attention now. "And?"

"So I tied Skye to a tree. All around this hole are some very little trees, but they're all bent over, all thin and spindly looking."

Manda stopped and took a deep breath. "It is really weird out there. It was completely quiet - the wind wasn't even blowing for a little while. I started feeling sort of creepy all by myself. Like I was being watched. I went down into the doorway."

"You should've come on back. It wasn't safe to go down there," Matthew told her, but gently. He could see it had really bothered her. Even more, he needed for her to tell him what this was. He did not know anything about it. And Matthew Rankin prided himself on knowing everything there was to know about everywhere he was.

"I wanted to know what the steps were for," Manda explained. "I thought I might not be able to find the place again. I mean, I've been riding all over this base, but never came across them before. So, I walked over to the steps. I didn't know they were a tunnel then. I thought maybe they were some kind of fancy foxhole, y'know, like the ones in the woods behind here."

Matthew nodded. Scattered all through the woods behind base housing were foxholes dug into the sandy earth, reinforced with notched and cross laid logs. Protection from the enemy all those years ago, just outside your door.

"So, anyway, I went to the steps and stood there for a minute. I had prickles on the back of my neck, like you do when someone is watching you. But that was silly. I was the only one out there. I decided that if I went down and saw what was there, I would feel better." She stopped. "So I went down the steps and there's sort of a little room, but then off to one side there is a doorway."

"And you went in it?"

Manda nodded. "Yep, for a few steps. But something growled at me. Once you get down the steps, the little room makes a roof over where you have to go to get into the tunnel. I couldn't see what it was. Sure sounded like a dog."

"You stopped there, I hope, when you couldn't see?" Matthew asked her, sharply, and then stopped himself. "What's in the part you saw?" he asked.

"Some pieces of what look like used to be barrels of stuff sitting on some wet ground. I imagine the rain runs in there." She said. "Anyway, the tunnel goes pretty much straight back. There are lots of doorways off of it. It reminded me of standing the in hall of a hotel. The floor is pretty bumpy and uneven."

She stopped as the front door slammed and Manda's younger brother yelled, "I'm home." The clatter of a hockey stick and skates thrown to the floor came next, and Matthew's momentary thread to his daughter broke with the interruption.

Matthew hurried to finish, "For now, don't say anything about this, and don't go out there again. Not until I have a chance to check this out." He frowned at her to make his point.

"I'm guessing that you don't know anything about this?" Manda said. She liked to catch him at not knowing, like to pull at the idea of limits and commands. He sighed. A soldier she would never make.

"I don't," he nodded. "But I want to find out what it is. Now, no more said, and no more riding out there." He paused and looked at her. "This time I want you to do as I say."

Manda lowered her head so that her hair fell over her eyes, watching him for a moment.

She nodded.

Chapter 10

On Tuesday, a week after Manda's news, Matthew put the last paper in his outbox just as his desk clock chimed thirteen hundred hours. He sat for a minute, thinking about his afternoon plan to check into what Manda had found. He signed off on the night duty orders and told his secretary Jean he would be out of touch that afternoon.

She nodded and went back to her typing. A surprise inspection of the base was rumored to be on deck. Today would be a good day to do an unannounced pre-check on their readiness, so when the federal inspectors came in two weeks the base would be up to par. And if Matthew didn't tell her where he was going she could honestly not pass it on.

He checked out a jeep from the motor pool, and angled across the base past the old hospital and guard dog cemetery. Going this way kept him out of the main traffic area, where rotaries connected the PX and runway traffic with that of the main gate. He did not want anyone to see him out and about. This side of the base was shut down due to federal cutbacks, and few vehicles moved along these roads. It also took him across the firing range, where Manda said she had ridden that day.

Matthew turned off the pavement and downshifted. The jeep whined into a lower gear as he bumped off of the pavement, following a trace of wheel marks in the short roadside grass. The Cape did not have much underbrush, and roads, once cleared, tended to remain a long, long time.

He drove slowly until he saw a screen of trees and rocks. It fit the description Manda had given him. Manda would not have ridden Skye any farther into the rocks than she first reported, he knew. She was that careful of her mare's legs.

He rolled to a stop as he cut the engine and listened. Nothing. Not a bird, no sound of car or boat. He stepped out of the jeep and looked around. He settled his two-way radio on his belt and began walking. She had said she thought she was heading toward the bay, that the hospital had been to her left and behind her when she had last seen its roofline in the distance. His eyes swept the trees in front of him.

It was just as Manda had described, a few spindly trees and some piles of rock. The smell of pine came to him faintly from the far off tree line, the old, settled, warm and spicy smell of late afternoon. Bits and pieces of metal lay about on the ground. He looked more closely. Some were the rims of old barrels, left long after the thin sides were gone, and many were the casings and shells of spent bullets and warheads.

He turned in a one-eighty and suddenly caught sight of a pile of wood and sand. He turned back again to look. Yes, that might be it. He was farther along than she had been when he left the road. Small trees hid the groundswell so that he did not know it was there until he was almost standing on it.

He started to make his way through the sand, then stopped and frowned down at his uniform shoes, clean and brightly polished. He should have changed into his boots, but they were back in the jeep. He wavered, then shrugged and moved on. He just wanted a quick look-see.

Manda's tale had seemed strange. It would only take a minute, was probably nothing but a cellar hole or storage site. He walked around the last groundswell and stopped. In front of him was the doorway she had spoken of, cut back into the hill. Whatever this had been, it went back in quite a way.

He thought back to all the papers that had been given to him on taking this assignment. The outgoing commander, a longserver just finishing his tour, had laughed at Matthew's thoroughness at reading all the material. "I never did all that looking back, just kept to the day-to-days. This base isn't much noticed anymore." Matthew nodded and had not argued. Silence got you a lot, he had learned. There was no need to quarrel with a general. But he had read at night, anyway.

Now he could not remember any mention in the base plan books and exercise journals of a notation about this part of the base being used for storage or anything else. He looked again and decided to get his flashlight from the jeep. He made his way back and grabbed the light, flicking it on into his cupped hand to check the batteries and beam.

He rounded the rise again and stopped short. A man stood just beyond the opening, bent and holding a tissue to his nose, intent upon a rush of blood he was trying to stem.

Matthew's thoughts processed with typical speed; intruder, older, male, jacket one shade lighter than his own Air Force blue windbreaker, and first aid was needed. He wondered where the man had come from. He had heard no other car, seen no one else moving on his slow way in.

"Here, take this." He approached the man with his handkerchief proffered, flapping in the afternoon sun. The man started and backed up two sudden steps, as un-nerved as Matthew at finding someone else in this quiet place.

"No, am all right. All right." A faint accent flavored the words. The man quit bleeding as he straightened up. Matthew studied his visitor curiously. The man was a good bit older than himself, with muscles defined and hard from use. His hair was clipped short, blond gone gray, soft and faded colors against which his eyes were a startling, clear blue.

The immediate crisis past, he moved to the next item on the agenda. "You are on closed land," he began. "This is an Air Force base. It is not open to civilians."

"Yes, sorry." The man stepped back. "I will go now." Matthew nodded and watched the man make his way back to the trees beyond the tunnel entrance. In a few minutes his figure was lost in the shadows. Matthew listened for a moment but heard no sounds of anyone returning. The man must have left the area.

He moved on down toward the tunnels and pulled the flashlight from the pocket of his light jacket. The shallow steps were rock, scuffed in the middle from the foot traffic they had once handled. He put a hand on the overhang as he made the last step down, then picked his way carefully through some sort of sludge to a dry spot a few feet into the tunnel. Here he flicked on the flashlight and played it across the tunnel opening. The light bounced off the rock walls and the doorways Manda had mentioned.

Silence met him, a heavy one, and he stopped to listen. There are different kinds of silences he had learned in his years of secrets. Of dying, of giving up, of something no longer used. This one spoke of emptiness now, but not of never being entered. You could feel the charge in the air. He could smell the dank, wet scent of animal, too. To the left were the barrels Manda had mentioned.

He moved forward, passing doorways to his left and right, a series of small rooms. In the outside walls he noticed small, grilled openings set between the rooms' doors. His beam swept further into the dark. At his waist the two-way radio squawked with a bit of static. The rock of these tunnels cut the signal all but dead. He moved further into the tunnel, playing the light ahead of him.

He emerged as dark was settling and walked back to his jeep. A curious place, not used nor walked through for years, but once it had been something busy. You could tell from the traces of walkways and faint squares of building foundations that more than a few people had once been here. But this old base was full of shut and shuttered places that he was still learning about. He pulled the jeep back onto the main road and headed home.

Matthew entered his office the next morning and said good morning to Jean. As usual, she had arrived before him, driving from her home in the small town of Cohasset. Her whole career had been on this base. That said a lot for her abilities, both with paper and people, because generals are notoriously picky and usually want to hire their own staff. This morning she brought him coffee and a stack of classified communications that the night duty officer had pulled off of the Telex. Matthew began to go through them, and as he initialed and shuffled them into priority order, he asked,

"Jean, I'm pretty new at New England history, being from Texas and all."

She nodded. Her family had been among the first in the area and still lived here among bits and pieces of the past. On weekends she was a docent at the living history display at Plymouth Rock.

"Is there any kind of history on the base?" he asked.

She thought, "Not a lot. This part of the Cape was scrub and marsh. The government bought it back in the '20s and started different kinds of operations back then. I don't know much about them, though. It wasn't until World War II that the base really geared up and grew so large. I guess if you find any history, that would be the time it would come from." She shrugged. "That, of course, really isn't old enough by New England standards to be interesting. It just sort of is." She gathered the papers into a pile, neatly knocking them on the desk edge until they were perfectly even. Another thing the generals liked.

She paused at the door, searching for any other details. "It was a prisoner of war camp," she said. "There were about eighteen hundred prisoners here for about a year, more or less."

Matthew did not recall any mention of that at all.

"More or less?" he asked her. "What kind of POWs?"

"Germans," she answered briefly. "Taken when things began to go our way in Europe, I expect. At least that's where they came from." She moved toward the door. "I haven't thought of that in years," she said. "No one ever mentions it."

"Thank you," he said, as if it were a little matter. "I didn't know we had German POWs here."

She nodded and went on out, the topic discussed and put to rest. She was an excellent secretary, not given to wasting time. Matthew pulled his daybook toward him on the desk, ready to begin working. On today's square he penciled a question mark, very lightly.

****

Two weeks later a report of wild dogs sent Matthew far out on the base again. He drove through the bright fall afternoon, in and out on many small dirt roads, but had seen no sign of dogs when he realized he was near the tunnels again. On a whim, he swung in and parked. The dim solitude and dampness of them had stayed in his mind. In his few unbusy moments, he had wondered at the particulars of what the place had been. But he had done nothing more to look into it.

Now he changed into old boots and set off quietly from behind the slight rise to the left of the tunnels. The sand crunched satisfactorily under his feet, and the wind blew today with the soft warmth Indian summer brings. He forgot sometimes that such days lay beyond his office walls.

He walked to the middle of the road, just tracks in the sand now, and stood looking. In bright daylight the disuse stood out even more in detail. But he began to see a pattern.

The sun dropped a bit, and he shaded his eyes and began to walk toward the tunnel doorway up ahead. As he approached it, he looked around and smiled. It was all so familiar. Such rocks marked the walkways and edges of the base he ran now. Cedar posts were still the foundations of the buildings and barracks used by the people he commanded. More four-corner post patterns here and there, more traces of walkways to what must have been other places to go.

Now, knowing what had been, he could see the winding path of the perimeter fence that gapped just in front of him, where the main road from the base had come in. The once-driven area lay flat and smooth, with tufts of grass beginning to soften its lines.

Large smooth stones still lay in straight lines if you knew where to look. A few still had a shading of white on their sides. Those would have been the edges of paths between the buildings.

A faint scraping sound caught his ear, and back in the trees a flash of blue moved from sun to tree shadow almost before he saw it. The same blue as the windbreaker of the man he'd seen here before.

Coincidence made Matthew Rankin nervous. Got his attention, as it were. The nature of his job was suspicion. Correctly placed and energetically enforced, it kept at bay the things that could undermine his country. He firmly believed that, but he did not believe in coincidence. Not innocent and by chance, anyway.

As if reading his thoughts, the sounds moved away from him somewhere in the trees. But pilots' eyes are quick, reactions even quicker, and Matthew moved more swiftly toward the sound than the maker could hasten away. Or rather, the runner had meant to hasten. But as the last time, speed brought blood in a rush, and he'd bent double to stem the flow when Matthew came upon him.

"Here," he ordered and grabbed an arm to push the man to kneeling, offering a handkerchief with the other hand. At first the man struggled, then coughed once, closed his eyes and bled copiously until the white square was drenched to the very edges. Matthew held him, more gingerly now, and tried to fix an age on his trespasser. Not as old as he had first thought, maybe near sixty.

Dusk had fallen around them with a swiftness that always surprised him. He looked down at the grayed hair and felt an old locked bit of memory stir. This man was probably the age his father would be if he were still alive. *How odd*, he thought, *to think of that just now*. He didn't think much about his father, who had died alone, by choice.

Matthew put those memories firmly back where he kept them, barricaded behind thought of any kind, and made ready to deal with this man who oughtn't to be on his Air force base.

He waited patiently for the man to ease up, signaling that the crisis was past.

"You're here twice," said Matthew.

"Walking."

"No." He shook his head. "Not in this place."

The man looked again and seemed to contemplate his response. Above them the wind sighed, and he grew almost impatient. It would not do to have no answer, yet this man did not seem to be willful.

Matthew went back a step. "Your name?"

Again he waited, but the silence grew into moments that stretched and thinned with expectation, like a rubber band that might snap any moment and lay a red mark across your wrist.

"Jan," the man said at last. "My name is Jan."

Matthew studied the speaker. There was a tone, a reluctance that made him wonder at the truth beneath the words. He picked a next step that was helpful, most of all to himself.

"I'll take you home," he said.

Jan nodded faintly, the movement just visible in the now full dark. Matthew's eyes adjusted to the night, and the shape of the jeep swam from the dark, its roll bar and headlights glowing eerily in the moonlight. He considered, and then rose and walked swiftly to the jeep. Matthew drove slowly, the headlights dipping and bouncing as he eased to a stop beside the timbers Jan rested against.

Moving to the man's side, he bent and gathered him up as Jan struggled to help himself rise. He lifted him into the jeep and got back behind the wheel breathing hard and with his heart bumping in his chest hard enough to remind him that he too was no longer as fit as the young captain he had been.

He watched his passenger, who waved weakly toward the trees. Matthew shifted into first and eased down a stretch of road he hadn't driven before. This edge of the base ended in a ravine. Sand tracks wound through the trees, and Matthew frowned while easing the jeep in and up out of the ruts washed by runoff rain. A turn to the right brought them through more trees and then out a short way to a paved road. Pines pressed close on either side, and he thought once again how the trees hid away things that were really quite near to each other.

He sat for a moment to get his bearings, left to the base gate, right into Falmouth. The corpsman at the base emergency room went off duty at sixteen hundred hours, and it was long past that now. So town it would be, he decided, and turned right. In town was Will Sustine, a reservist physician who ran a clinic. With luck he would still be there, wrapping up his day.

Matthew opened his mouth to say as much when the man groaned and the bleeding came anew. This time dizziness became unconsciousness and Matthew cursed as he kept a hand on the swaying shoulder, making town in record time.

Chapter 11

The Jeep's wheels whispered on the paved road as the headlights bounced off trees pressed close on either side, their branches reaching overhead. Jan rested his head back on the seat as the lights of Falmouth passed by.

Matthew took the first right turn off the rotary. Silver Beach Road ran straight on to the ocean. Down its length the headlights picked up a small, gray-shingled house at the end of the road. Behind it, long, salt grass rippled and swayed, then gave way to the rim of Silver Beach itself and the dark space of the ocean.

In that house, Will Sustine, a reservist, had the town's one medical practice. A competent redhead, he and Matthew had a brusque working relationship. Matthew knew him to be a good doctor through weekends when Sustine served as a major in the Massachusetts National Guard.

As Matthew had expected, Sustine was there finishing up his records for the day when Matthew helped Jan up the stairs and into the front room of the clinic.

"Bleeding again," Sustine said, and transferred Jan's weight from Matthew's shoulder to his own. His eyes met

Matthew's briefly. "Let me see what's up." He shifted Jan gently, and they disappeared down a hallway to the three exam rooms and Sustine's office.

Matthew peeled off his jacket and looked around, curiously. He had not been here before. The office was simple and old-fashioned, all oiled, good wood furniture with a rock fireplace and woven baskets for patient magazines.

A wide, shuttered window banked one wall that must look out on the bay during the day. Tonight it was just black. A bell tolled somewhere off the beach, an easy ringing that spoke of slow swells in a quiet sea.

He took a seat in the row of straight-backed wooden chairs that lined the white-walled room. He picked up a magazine, but didn't see the words on the page as he thought about what would be going on in his house right now. He liked it every night when he pulled up and the windows glowed with yellow light in the Cape's early dark. Inside, something would probably be bubbling on the stove or in the oven.

This colder clime had set Ginny to fixing stews and casseroles; steamy, hearty foods they ate at the table with the fireplace flickering behind them.

He thought briefly of calling home, but then decided against it. Ginny was used to her husband's uncertain schedule and absences.

He closed his eyes and listened to Sustine's voice echoing in the exam room down the hall. Sometimes a quieter voice mingled in, the tone diffident and explaining. He could not make out the words, but Sustine's tone sounded patient. Matthew rubbed his eyes, feeling the graininess of fatigue he would rarely admit to.

At length came the sound of a door being opened and Sustine's heavy tread came down the hall. He appeared in the doorway and jerked his head, motioning Matthew to come with him.

In the first exam room, a lamp in the corner cast a glow much homier than the bright white one directly over the bed where Matthew's charge lay. Breaking a sealed IV pack, Sustine reached for an outstretched arm and Jan obliged, eyes closed and breathing shallow. Sustine swabbed the inside bend of the elbow, raised a blue vein and and slid a needle in, then watched for a moment to see that the blood welled. He reached up and turned a knob on the IV pole, and a drip slid down the long tube and was sucked up by the needle. He taped it and laid the arm gently on top of the white, woven blanket.

On Jan's wrist a raised blue lump ran for two inches up the inside of the wrist. Sustine ran a thumb along it. Hard and fibrous, ridged, almost calcified.

He glanced at Matthew and back at the mark, but didn't say anything. "We'll leave you to rest now a bit," he said, and the slight figure on the bed nodded once.

Sustine led Matthew back to the waiting area where they took two seats in the row against the wall. Sustine sighed, ""He's bleeding pretty badly, but it has slowed up," he said. "It hasn't changed except to get a little worse over the years."

Matthew raised his eyebrows. "You know who he is then? This is not a new thing?"

"No, no. I've been treating Jan Neuman for years," Sustine said. "I don't have anything I can give him more of here. The problem is the bleeding. He's coming in contact with something so caustic it ruptures the capillaries in his airways. But you can't make a man be treated. I won't, anyway. So he comes when it's needed and not between.

"His blood counts are very erratic, sometimes really high. Other times they look more normal. I've run the few tests we can do here, but we're rural and limited. I've not come to any conclusions, and we just can't do any more diagnosing with the equipment we have." He studied Matthew, "I'm on the edge confidentiality wise here, but he may need some help, and he's never put down a next-of-kin."

Matthew digested that, arms crossed, watching the fire as it flickered into embers and grayed around the edges. He changed the subject.

"You brought that scar on his arm to my notice," he said, mildly.

"That mark is odd," he said. "I've only seen it before in inmates who had escaped and tried to obliterate a tattoo. They shoot up with bleach just under the skin to eat away at the tattoo. Can make you sick as a dog, but eventually it works."

He glanced at the clock on the wall. "You'll be wanting to get home tonight. There's not more we can do for him. I'll keep him overnight." Sustine's own small house sat behind the clinic at the corner of the parking lot, on the last alley before the beach.

They moved back to the exam room, and Matthew watched Will do a new check of vitals.

"Temp's down, and your pulse and blood pressure," he said to Jan. "I'd like to keep you here for the night, see how you are in the morning."

"No." Jan shook his head. "I do not wish to stay in anyplace not my own," he said. "Not while I am able to go home."

"I'll take him home, Will." Matthew volunteered. "You've helped quite a bit tonight, already." *And*, he thought, *I'll find out where this man lives*. He looked back at the man in the bed and found he was also being studied, the blue eyes said, *I know why you want to take me*. For a moment their eyes locked, then Jan gave a slight nod.

"That would be most welcome," he said. Sustine shrugged, disconnected the IV, and Matthew helped his visitor into the jeep and waited for directions. The man coughed again and motioned Matthew forward. They drove back out toward the base. Matthew watched the headlights coming towards them, wondering where this drive might end. Sustine had disturbed him with the information that there was of no known next-of-kin, as though he, Matthew, might take on the care of this man.

An hour later found Matthew driving slowly through the hamlet of Rachel's Corner and turning down a sandy track toward the trees. The wheel ruts ran slightly downhill from the paved road, and the car lights at last shone on a small cottage backed by a barn to the right and the sheen of flat, smooth water beyond. He studied the cottage, sturdy and well built.

Straight out to the back lay the blackness of the ocean, strung along the edges with lights. Out here they looked like a scatter of pearls strewn in a semicircle across the dark. Somewhere a foghorn brayed, then there came the long distant bellow of a freighter's stack.

The Georgia banks had caught and caused a thousand shipwrecks in two hundred years, and any night could bring one thousand and one.

"Here is good." Jan motioned for Matthew to stop.

The jeep rolled to a gentle halt in front of the steps to the porch. The old man coughed again, hanging onto the windshield for support. When he stopped, his breathing was ragged and harsh in the quiet of the clearing.

Jan slid one leg to the ground and stood shakily upright, grasping the seat's edge.

"I thank you," he said, then began walking slowly toward the steps. Once more Matthew tried to place the slight inflection but a naming wouldn't come.

"Rest now," he told Jan, and backed the jeep away. He was curious about the man, but asking would have to come later. He had learned that you find the most when no one knows you are looking. He shifted into first and drove up the hill toward home.

Two more times over the next week, Matthew made the drive between the trees. Once with a few purchased items, the other with just himself. Each time there seemed to be little to find out about this man. He lived quietly at the end of the small lane and farmed cranberries from the two bogs just beyond the house. On the surface, anyway.

****

It's funny what a little kindness can do, like nursing along a stubborn old lock. You keep at it, coaxing a little more with each effort yet stopping before it breaks. The frozen stubborn ones give way at last and give up what they kept inside. Sometimes the secrets are for telling others; sometimes they are things we have kept even from ourselves.

****

Jan began to watch the red taillights disappear at the end of Matthew's visits. He sighed a deep shuddering breath, drawing air down into a part of his lungs where he'd held his breath for years. He'd forgotten the sweet, clean tang of pine-kissed oxygen when you breathed down to your toes. He realized that he had not breathed so little because of being ill, but because he had been afraid to breathe.

To live.

It is said that we create our own aloneness, sometimes, anyway. That hesitation makes others not see the part of us that most needs for someone to. How can it be that thirty years can go by at such a quiet pace? How can a man lay unnoticed, yet have always been amid others and still be all alone?

Chapter 12

M atthew mounted the three steps and opened the door to his office the next morning. Three more strides brought him to his secretary's desk, a scarred, honey wood that sat centered on the wall behind it.

"Good morning, Jean," he greeted her. To the left side of her desk a small table held a pot of fresh coffee and thick, white china mugs. Just past that was his office door. To the right of her desk were the conference room and a wall of photos of jets and generals.

"Good morning, Colonel," she responded, her words clipped and pleasant. She stood and picked up a stack of manila folders and phone messages atop a bright blue file marked Daily Folder.

Matthew poured himself a cup of the strong, black brew and went into his office. Jean poured her own and followed him in, placing the papers and folders on the desk between them. She pulled a chair close and they worked their way through the pile, setting the agenda for the day.

Efficiently she made two stacks, her own and one for Matthew's attention. That done, she pushed back her chair and rose to go.

As she reached the door, he asked her, "Where are the old personnel records?"

"None here in this office except for the active men," she replied. "In the old training hangar at the far end of the runway, there are former base records. Personnel files are stored there when a man is deactivated."

He nodded his thanks, and she went out.

He looked at his day's obligations and put a star next to twelve hundred hours. Noon. Then he pulled his stack of dailies in front of him and began to list on a lined tablet the motor pool schedule for the week.

Matthew Rankin's first principle of searching was that you learned a lot when no one knew you were looking. The second was to know what you did not know. And the third, grown from the first two, was to surprise people with what you knew at a moment they didn't expect. That might give you more info than you had already, albeit involuntarily.

At twelve hundred hours - noon, Air Force time - he headed for the training hangar on the far side of the runway. The tarmac sent up heat shimmers that made the building look as if it sat pooled in a mirage.

He parked his jeep on the wide expanse of concrete in front of the huge sliding doors that were padlocked and chained closed. Once this hangar had bustled with men and planes and the radio traffic of their coming and goings. Now he sat and listened to the wind whistle in the empty places, calling for something no longer there.

He shook his head and brought his thoughts back to the task at hand, then sorted through the keys on his ring. A tab of shiny black electrical tape marked the one he wanted. The metal building had dulled to a flat, dark gray in the salt and cold over the years. The windows were grimed, and somewhere a loose bit of metal screeched in the wind. He selected the taped key and moved to the staff door to the left of the big hangar doors. The lock was stiff, and he worked the key back and forth until the hasp grated open.

He stepped inside. The air was chill and smelled of not having been stirred for a long time. Not much was left in the office - two old brown chairs with torn seats, a gray metal desk, and a black four-drawer filing cabinet. He pulled the drawers open, one by one, searching quickly through the sparse files left behind. In the second one he found a clipboard that listed boxes by number, with a date and scrawled signature of the deliverer. He passed on through the small office and briefing room and into the darkened part of the hangar.

His footsteps echoed in the space, and he stopped for a minute, breathing in the scent of oils and metals that lingered. *Some things don't change much*, he thought; the two hangars that serviced the fighter jets still on the base had the same smell.

He was looking for records, though, and walked on into the darkness until he found the stack of boxes on the other side of the hangar. A rudimentary pallet system for the records had been set up in a corner.

Matthew went back into the old briefing room and pulled the clipboard from the drawer of the filing cabinet, then returned to the rows of boxes. Older records were stored to the rear and he found the '40s along the outer wall, the boxes tattered but still whole.

The cartons were dusty and within minutes his hands and jacket were covered with a fine, gray film. The personnel records were kept by service date and alphabetically within tours dates. He sighed and began looking, shuffling folders that were old and soft on the corners and slid away from his fingers.

He discovered records for forty years of base history and sorted through them by tab and binder label. There were man-days reports, platoon lists, motor pool records, flight logs, mess records and recipes, housing lists and supply requisitions in the first boxes. He looked at the heap of boxes and sighed, it would be a long afternoon. He had promised himself he would read every name he came across.

Six hours later he had been through them all. He stopped, wiping his face with the last clean part of a handkerchief and thought for a moment. There was no one named Jan Neuman in any of the records.

He turned back and was closing the flaps on the last box when a bulky brown envelope caught his eye. Camp Penn was written in faded black across the face. He pulled it out and laid it to the side, restacking the last box tight against the next row.

He crossed back to the flight office with the camp records in hand. Late afternoon sun shafted across the desks and onto the dusty blackboard on the wall. He settled down at the first desk, spreading the records out before him.

Outside, tires squealed to a quick halt and a voice called, "Colonel Rankin? We have an alert! Plane in distress!"

Matthew pushed the papers back into their envelope, tucking it under his arm. He left the hangar at a trot, ready for the possible emergency an alert could bring. Most often these jet scares came to nothing, but it only took once to crash.

The bright sunlight caught on dust motes swirling in the air as the door slammed shut. He snapped the lock shut on the hasp and ran to his jeep.

As the sergeant swung the jeep around, Matthew pulled his own in close behind, and they headed for the runway.

Inside his jacket, the heavy envelope rested stiff against his chest.

It was the next morning before he opened the first folder and found a penciled map of Camp Penn. He pulled it out and studied the layout of the camp buildings and roads. Paper-clipped to it was a pencil sketch on graph paper of the camp buildings, with neat writing listing inventories and activities inside each room.

Those were interesting, but even more interesting was the location. At one end was a dark square marked storage tunnels. Manda's tunnels.

She had by chance found the old POW camp when she was riding. He read on. Camp Penn had been built as a satellite camp for Hanscom Air Field, in Boston.

Then he turned to the last pages and stopped. There lay a list of prisoners by name and rank of originating field unit in the German army. The top pages were typed and neat. Behind them were original pages, columns of names and numbers written in many hands. Scrawled, crossed out and almost unreadable, the notes appeared to track the prisoners' comings and goings. He paged quickly through them to the N's and looked for Neuman, Jan, but with no luck.

The war had ended in '45. But the list of names and dates in his hand held names as late as '47, catalogued by date and unit and battle of capture, transport ship, entry point and personal identification number. The pages were torn and dirty, but they did show the changes made to the prisoner count.

Outside his door a voice sounded and he jumped. Beside him lay a sheaf of orders to be signed and the night officer's log to be completed. Either could also easily cover this map if someone should walk in. He wasn't sure what he was hiding - maybe his own confusion.

He looked again at the busy drawings, then glanced at his watch. It was time to go. He carefully folded the map and tucked it and the lists into a fresh envelope with nothing written across its surface. Now that he knew what had been there, he wanted to look at the prison camp traces again.

Matthew drove his own car this time, an old, white station wagon that swayed as it took the sandy track back to the small trees. The shocks and brakes were soft and loose as he drove into the ruts. He rolled to a stop and got out to look with map in hand.

He found the tunnels, turning the map so that the mark for the gate on the paper matched the opening between the two slight rises that stood in front of him. He began to walk slowly, matching bits of road and foundation to the key of buildings and roads within the camp.

It was an old, desolate place. He stood and wondered, *what would an old man be doing there*? Rule Number One: look in the little places first for your proof and reasons. Was there something here that someone sought?

****

He would not have thought it so hard to find a man. He sighed as he hung up from his last phone call. None of his efforts had produced a Jan Neuman, much less a medical history to help Will Sustine treat him. The town records held no help - one year he was there, and the year before he was not listed in the cross-x phone books of the library.

Matthew used his Air Force contacts to have a search made for medical records under that name by either state or federal benefits. It was as if Jan Neuman had not been anywhere before he lived in Rachel's Corner.

The last place he checked was the prison system, calling the warden with the question of how could a man be found.

"Such requests for identification are usually passed to me," he explained to Matthew. "To answer your question, no, we do not mark our people with their past, Mr. Rankin. When they have served their time they are free to begin again as best they can." The voice was cool. "May I ask what this is about?"

Matthew gently disconnected then. He did not have an answer. He stared at his list of crossed out items. Rule Number Two: Know what you do not know. The other side of which is, know what you know it is not.

He said nothing to Will Sustine about what he had not found, because that third rule on the list of rules of searching was that you also never gave away what you did not know.

****

Matthew threaded his car through the turns in the soft road just outside Rachel's Corner for the second time in as many weeks.

Between the trees he caught glimpses of the ocean's blue and the bogs that lay holding berries waiting to be flooded when the winter's cold set in. The small cottage appeared suddenly in its clearing. From up above on the road, he hardly noticed that it was there.

"Greetings." Jan came from the barn with a rake in hand. "I am just now bedding down the horses."

"When you're finished, I'd like to talk to you." Matthew stood and waited.

"Yes, sure." Jan turned walked back to put the rake inside the tack room doorway. Matthew studied him as he did. A stocky, older man with graying hair and shoulders more bowed than once, probably. Moving better than the last time he'd seen him.

"Let's go inside." Jan led Matthew to the kitchen door. From the stove a smell of meat and onions filled the air with a rich scent

"Yes? Tea?" Jan motioned him to a chair at the table and took one across from him. On the back of the stove a teapot stood, its spout trickling steam.

Matthew nodded to the drink and said, "Will Sustine worried about how to treat you. He isn't sure what might be wrong."

"It is no matter. I am better these last few days." Jan reached to pour some tea and his arm stretched brown and corded and hard in front of Matthew. The blued scar ran up his arm, white and fibrous except for the last bit, which ran darkly across the muscles. It was an X if you looked hard enough, stretched by corded muscle and sinew and efforts to obliterate it, but an X just the same. He turned away to gather milk and sugar and spoons to stir the tea.

Matthew pulled the envelope out of his pocket and laid it on the table. Jan Neuman turned back and saw it, a small stack of yellowed pages with lists of names and numbers.

Jan did not move, went beyond quiet into still, seeming not to breathe. Matthew reached out then and touched the blued scar, raising an eyebrow at Jan.

Jan faltered the teapot back to the table and sat back in his chair.

"My number, yes, is on that list. But, no, not upon my arm. There are no X's on that list," Jan Neuman said. "The X, I did, to hide the number that was there."

Matthew was motionless in his chair. Out of breath, as if he had run a race. Rules One and Three: Details in the smallest place and do not tell what you do not know.

Jan Neuman was a German national. *No, he was a Nazi.*

Behind Jan the fire popped and sparks rolled across the floor to his feet, but he didn't look at them. Matthew stared at him. Jan swallowed and lifted his eyes from the floor and met it. *How can you be what you are?*

Matthew's eyes were full of distaste. Jan's stomach roiled. *How indeed?* He had often thought that he did not know who he was either.

He looked back at the floor.

Jan Neuman had always known this day would come.

He had thought about it with dread for years, but now that he seemed to be dying, did it matter so very much? Had it ever? Somewhere deep inside, it almost felt like peace, this having been found out.

"I know what you are," said Matthew, his voice cutting.

"No," said Jan. "You cannot know that, because I do not either."

Chapter 13

"W hy?" Matthew asked. "Why are you still on the base?"

Jan opened his eyes again and met Matthew's gaze. He shifted in his chair and turned his head away, looked at the whorls within the woodgrain of the table, sighed and spoke at last.

"I look because of the tunnels," came the answer, the voice soft and worn.

Matthew moved his chair closer. "Again," he said.

Jan drew a deep breath and said, "I have not always come there. It is not something I wish to remember, being a prisoner."

Matthew stared at him in disbelief. "You were fighting our country," he said. "You're lucky you were alive to be a prisoner."

Jan bowed his head briefly, then said, "You asked to hear this."

"Go on." Matthew sat back.

"Lately, these last years, I grew more sick, and I recalled a rumor, a story, of something maybe left there that could help me get well. No one comes here, and I think perhaps this thing is still there. These items, coins could maybe be traded for money.

I look because I am sick and I need to see a doctor. And to do that here, in this country, is to have the money to pay for it." He stopped and coughed again and looked past Matthew to something only he could see.

"When I became a prisoner here everything was busy and crowded. There were many planes and many troops. We were kept at many camps, moving often. And we came here after being in Maine, where we helped with the logging in the forest.

"So many prisoners in and out, and not all men are the same. Some are more hungry, some crave smokes…"

"And what was used to acquire these things?" Matthew interrupted.

The old man stopped speaking and took a sip of his tea.

"Cigarettes, extra rations, a watch, a ring, coins that were not found when we were searched. Matches, especially matches, chocolate bars." He took another drink and suddenly began to talk along a whole new line.

"They put up this camp in a hurry, when your country changed the tide of the war. There were many prisoners to be taken out of the way so that the progress of winning could continue across Europe. When we first came here there were live shells and many already spent ones lying about. Where the camp was put had been something before."

"Like?" Matthew prompted. He jiggled his foot, impatient with this new story.

"For practicing your guns and explosives. These tunnels that are there, they were used for purposes other than prisoners. The tunnels were used as a last resort when some altercations began to occur between us, the prisoners."

"About?"

Jan sighed. "Some months into my stay at this camp, here, a group of Afrika Korps came." Jan looked at Matthew's face. It did not change, so he added, "They were some of the most zealous, most believing of Hitler's troops. Once we were here, away from the war, many of the German soldiers began to not be as much believers as they had been. They had served Hitler because of their loyalty to their country, not really to the idea of Nazism. This irked the Afrika troops who were loyal still.

"One of the town men came and taught us English. He made us read children's books because he said that the very simple words and phrases were things we could easily began to understand and recognize." Jan smiled slightly. "We were going to read Beauty and the Beast, but the man who taught said he thought we had had enough teaching about monsters for quite awhile.

"I remember how quiet it got, so still you could have cut the air with a knife. We all knew that by the monster that he meant the German side of the war.

"No one knew what to say, so, for once, no one said anything. But later, the Afrika Korps prisoners threatened some of the class members because they had not stood up and argued with the teacher.

"So they moved some of the troublemakers to the tunnels, to try and separate the fighting. But it did not work, for in the daytime we shared classes and mealtime and activities.

"And then the men who were there began to bleed a lot. And they were taken away to be treated in American hospitals. That was when the camps began to be separated. The Nazi soldiers went back to one of the bigger camps, the one in Boston, where there was more control and separation and they could be dealt with."

He stopped speaking.

"Were any of them punished?" Matthew asked.

"No, not that I saw. The people from the area were mostly kind. And like I say, that kindness was what really began to make us see that all the things we had been taught and told were not true." Jan hesitated.

"Go on, finish," Matthew urged.

"Well, we knew a cook and he said that he heard a man say at the officers' lunch that the bleeding might be from some barrels that were kept in the tunnels."

"Are you sure?" Matthew asked. "What was in the barrels? In the tunnels?"

Jan shrugged. "I do not know, but it was not something good, I think.

"It was a morning in the springtime. They came and got some of us who got along well with the Americans who worked at the camp. We took showers and got our clothes washed and pressed. Then we all got in a truck and drove to the runways. The plane landed and four men got off. Your base commander met them. There was a bugler there and flags flew."

Jan went on. "The men, three of them, were from Washington, D.C. One of them was high up in the branch that runs your troops. And the other two worked for him. They all got in a car and drove out to the camp, followed by our truck of model prisoners."

"What did they do?" Matthew asked.

"They went out for about two hours with the base commander and the sergeant in charge of the firing range. Then, in the afternoon, they met with a doctor and some of the prisoners. They spent some time watching the sick men. Then they walked through and met more closely some of the men who had just arrived.

"I thought they were just inspecting our place. But when lunch was served, I was passing drinks at the table. I heard one of them say something that sounded totally different. That the very ill prisoners were always among that group."

"And that was?"

"That the chemicals were very caustic, they thought, and that it was a problem that the prisoner of war camp had been built right next to where the chemicals had been stored. Then one, the tall one in a suit, said that it might have been an accidental beginning but that it worked out okay. It would be okay. And they went away. And nothing else was ever said within my hearing. And also, they never did anything about the tunnels."

"And some of the men kept on becoming ill?" Matthew asked, his voice quiet.

"Oh, yes. Several of them were very ill. I also was sick at the very end. It was very sudden when one day they ordered all of us to pack our things, and within hours trucks came and we all were taken to other places." He looked at Matthew. "If you see a list of prisoners, you will see the transfers in and out. I had been very ill, and one day when they were moving prisoners, I just walked away. I heard a few whispers that they thought one of the prisoners had died from the bleedings. They could not find him, but they did not want that spoken of. And so that one man was not talked about." He shifted in his chair.

"But that day." Jan returned to the question of the tunnels. "The men left so suddenly that they could not gather all of their things. Some of the men kept their barter stock hidden away. One always spoke out that he had two sapphires and some coins that would see him right again, if he ever got home. So I have been thinking, lately, that perhaps those things are still there. So many have forgotten about this, maybe I can be the one to find it"

Matthew asked. "And his name, this man who walked away?"

"His name was Franz Becker." Jan's voice was gruff. He paused a second and went on. "Franz Becker," he said again, more softly. "It seems odd to speak that name, like when you speak of a person long missed, but longer not thought of."

Jan's fingers moved fitfully, grasping nothing.

"And that is how I came to be here," he said softly. "I have been Jan Neuman now for more than thirty years." His voice was quiet but firm. "There was nothing to go back to. I could not imagine going back to a country to try a build a life in the middle of a people who would never stop being German, no matter how much they were urged."

He looked at Matthew. "Germans do not change easily or well. If you went there today, you would most likely find regret for the losses of Germany, but you would also still find a lot of people who could not, or would not, admit that the war was wrong."

"Wrong?" Matthew asked.

"Wrong, yes. I came to see that it was wrong for so many people to blindly follow the teachings of one man. So completely that they had no thoughts of their own, mind you. That is what I am talking about. But also wrong to have stayed silent about it." He stopped speaking for a moment.

Matthew looked at the floor as Jan went on. "I don't think of myself as German anymore. I think of myself as a man. And it was not even forgivable, to ever have done the things my country has been found to do." He looked at Matthew.

"So I guess it is that I ran away, when the press to move the soldiers happened that day. I was trusted to go to the supply house. And I did, then I just kept walking."

Matthew stirred in his chair. "And no one knows you're here?"

"If they do, they have not come."

Matthew Rankin left the old man that night, picking up his cap and jacket and walking out. Inside him warred old and new, good and bad, what to do with this odd discovery of one man by another.

He made his way through beach grass to the sand, and for a while he stood and watched the sky over the ocean. The night was still and clear, with a late hour cease of wind.

Beyond him the sound of the waves coming ashore sloshed through the dark. He drove home slowly, savoring the stillness and the time to think.

The next night found him turning again into the soft drive, drawn on a return trip to the cottage. Matthew pulled up, and Jan walked slowly to greet him in front of the barn. He was up and about, but still had the thin, tight look of someone who doesn't have enough of himself anymore.

"Come in," he invited Matthew, and they passed into the kitchen. Jan stretched out an arm, as if perhaps to offer tea, and sank without a sound to the floor. By the time Matthew reached him across the little space, a pool of thick, red blood was deep and sticky around Jan. Matthew grabbed a nearby towel with one hand and the phone with the other. By the time he got the number dialed, the towel was soaked in his hand.

Will Sustine came quickly at Matthew's summons, headlights sweeping through the trees as he turned in from the road above. Inside he set up the small bedroom with medical instruments and monitors. He ran Jan another IV and took the patient's temperature and pulse until Jan moaned and slid into a sweated sleep.

Jan's huddled form barely lifted the sheet as Matthew and Sustine turned away and moved back into the kitchen. Towels sodden with blood lay in damp heaps across the floor. Sustine pulled a sheet of plastic from his bag and began to gather the towels into a pile in the middle.

Matthew silently drew a pail of hot water and dumped in a quart of alcohol he found under the sink. He plunged and rung the string mop, methodically swabbing along behind Sustine until the little kitchen was filled with the pungent scent.

"I can't do more for him. He's lucky you stopped by tonight." Will Sustine told Matthew. "He must go somewhere for treatment, or he is probably going to die."

He gazed for a moment out into the dark and said, "I can help you find a place, if that would make it easier. Maybe not close, so that quiet is more easily kept."

Sustine met Matthew's eyes at this last bit. *He knows*, thought Matthew, *he knows something*. Sustine gave an almost imperceptible nod.

First, do no harm, popped into Matthew's mind. The physician's credo. He understood, healer first, soldier second. Sustine gazed levelly at him for a moment, then turned to gather his things.

He said goodnight, leaving Matthew alone next to the sleeping form. He did not want this duty of caretaker. He did not even know why he had come back tonight.

Yet he sat. At length the figure on the bed stirred and licked his cracked lips.

"Ah." Jan Neuman saw Matthew, and closed his eyes again.

And Matthew knew that he would help this man.

****

He began the next morning with a fresh legal pad, two sharpened pencils and a mug of strong, black coffee curling steam into the air. Just two mornings after hearing Jan's tale, Matthew found himself far from the orderly path of discovery he had envisioned. In front of him, he had begun to lay notes in order, trying to follow the chain of events. He had created two rows of papers and spaces, like a game of gin rummy when nothing quite matched up. In the long night before, Matthew had thought about the avenues open to him. He was due in Washington, D.C. four days from now, as the base liaison to the Pentagon.

The fingers of the Pentagon stretched as far as Maine, and he had to report monthly on training activities, numbers of flights and the budget set for the base. They would look at his man-days program, his use of personnel to run the base. Each month the numbers got a little smaller, each year the belt got cinched a little tighter.

To that trip he would now add the need to get Jan Neuman to a doctor, timed so that it would not be noticeable that he was not quite where he should be, just a bit later than planned.

He wheeled his chair backwards and looked at the map of the Eastern Seaboard tacked on his wall. All the places strung like charms on a bracelet lain out north to south: Boston, Cape Cod, New York, Washington D.C.

He lifted the phone and called Will Sustine. "Okay," he said, "Help me find a name." Will was as good as his word. He called back with the name and address of a poison specialist within two hours.

"This man has seen some patients for me," he told Matthew. "He's expecting you, and he won't be officially seeing this one."

"In New York?" Matthew had read the address he had written down.

"Is that a problem?" Will asked.

"No, I just haven't been there in a very long time," Matthew responded. Not since he was fifteen.

Now he lifted the phone and called back to his childhood. At the other end of the line, the phone rang six times before being answered.

"Brooklyn." A New York voice spoke in the clipped accent he had grown up with. Memory flooded in suddenly, a sudden flash of a hot afternoon, headed on the crowded train to Jones Beach. He had breathed in time to the click of the wheels, hoping for the scent of the ocean to be stronger than that of the sweaty, stout woman who knitted determinedly even in the heat.

"Christmas scarf." She bobbed cheerfully at him, her shoulder bumping his with every stitch she took.

Matthew swam back to the present and stood for a moment, taking stock of the sudden memory. *Why such a strong remembrance.* Perhaps because he would be returning to the borough for the first time in thirty-odd years.

He shrugged. *We go back to our roots,* he thought, *when things become unknown. Sometimes, the answers most show themselves when we aren't looking for or at anything else.*

The connection clicked and he spoke to Will's contact.

"David Graves? My name is Matthew Rankin. I have a man that I have been told you will see." He listened and wrote directions on the lined tablet, how to find one of the small quiet hospitals on a leafy Brooklyn street, a place where war and poison are not part of the address.

Chapter 14

Will Sustine talked to Jan about the arrangements, and Matthew went on with his plans to clear time in his schedule without seeming to do so. He signed things for Jean, reviewed a promotion list to take to DC for approval, and counseled two soldiers for a scuffle in the mess hall. By noon the plans were made. At two, he shifted the old station wagon into first gear and rolled away from his office, headed to Sustine's practice for copies of Jan's records to take along.

How convenient it would have been if Manda had stayed on the other side of the base.

On Sunday morning, Matthew pulled into the cottage road in his own car; no one would comment on his driving it. The front door opened, and Jan came out and pulled it shut. He stood for a moment, staring at it, placing one palm flat to the surface before he turned and made his way to the car. In his hand was a small bag.

"Good morning," Matthew greeted him. "Is that all you are taking?" he nodded toward the bag.

"Yes, this is all."

Matthew stowed the bag in the back seat and pulled back onto the road. Boston was seventy-seven miles away. There they would catch the train to New York City, just another couple of passengers on a Sunday jaunt. The drive they made was quiet, one lost in sleep and the other in thought.

At last Jan stirred and opened his eyes, "We are where?" he asked.

Matthew answered him. Jan considered again. "I would like to tell you my story," he said, "of why I did what I did."

Matthew looked briefly his way. For the first time those blue eyes were unclouded and clear, and he thought that for a moment, he might get a glimpse of the man inside. "It would be a welcome thing," he said wryly. "But later, when you are better. For now, keep your strength."

They entered Boston's outlying towns, and Matthew took the highway to the main station and caught the 10:00 for New York. Jan followed him through the turnstile and into the train car to their seats. His breathing was labored and he looked pale. He settled into his seat and closed his eyes. They remained shut for the whole trip.

Their train hit the edge of New York's bulk long before they found the city. The sprawl of towns and people reached far north up Highway 29. The train slowed and stopped, and the loudspeaker blared and crackled overhead.

It seemed that track damage ahead meant no further progress. All passengers were shunted and shuttled to the subway that rode into Grand Central Station. There they could either take a cab or connect trains and head under the bay to Brooklyn.

They came up off of the track into the cavernous hall of Grand Central Station. Matthew stopped. He had last been in Grand Central in 1947 when its grand opening made every paper in the land.

Now it lay in front of him, gray and dark, the constellation ceiling smeared to almost black instead of the brilliant seagreen that had once backed its gold-painted star images.

Beside him, Jan shouldered his small duffle and they read signs above the tunnels to find the right connecting train. A rough hand shot between them, pulling hard on Jan. He stumbled and faltered.

"Becker, it is you!" A short man pounded on his shoulder. "I cannot believe to see you here."

The stranger turned and looked sharply at Matthew. Matthew had an impression, fleeting, of wariness behind the eyes, as the same hand now came his way. "Willi Prang," announced the newcomer. "I knew Becker many years ago. We are off to see the camp in Maine. We are seeing something of America after so much time."

He turned back to Jan. "I thought you dead. You have never been in touch since we were going home. But you must have heard, you must be on the way there, too." Willi Prang smiled at Jan, who smiled back a bit. Let silence cover.

He raised a camera. "A shot of the two of you," he said and pushed them together, then stepped back two paces. *Flash*! The picture shot out and he held it for a moment. "Another. One for each," he said. "These Polaroid cameras do not always do a good job." He snapped them twice again, while behind them people pushed for the 41st Street stairs.

"Willi!" A voice called from somewhere in the crowd.

"I must go, my group is leaving," Prang handed them the second shot and went on his way, the quiet pulsating behind him.

"Of all the luck," said Jan. "To run into him here."

"Well, too late now." Matthew answered. They joined the press of people exiting to the street above and caught a cab to take them across the Bay into Brooklyn. Beside him Jan wobbled and Matthew grasped his arm

In Brooklyn's heart, Matthew's own squeezed tight and held so for a moment. These were his streets, his row houses, all from another life left long ago. Brooklyn, the only one of the five boroughs to not want tall buildings.

The hospital was a row house with grilled windows, built in the early 1900's by a prosperous merchant. The door opened to a buzzer, and inside were soft, light colors and tables with magazines.

David Graves turned out to be square and brusque, much like Will Sustine, whose roommate he had been at Columbia. He came to meet Jan and look over the file of numbers Matthew brought with him, blood counts and pressures and a history of bleedings. He read the folder in silence and then looked at Jan over the top of the manila folder. "You are sick. But we'll see what can be done. I'm thinking six weeks for you here."

Jan looked startled, but merely nodded. *It would have to be, it seemed.*

"I'll be back for him then," Matthew said to Graves, "Unless you contact me before."

He shifted his gaze to Jan, and for a moment their gaze held.

"Get better," Matthew said simply, and put his hand on Jan's forearm, just where the blue scar lay beneath his shirtsleeve. Jan looked hard at Matthew for an instant, then gave a sharp nod in answer.

Matthew and Graves shook hands, and Matthew went down the steps to the street, already headed back to his world.

****

On Monday, from LaGuardia, Matthew hopped a commuter flight bound for D.C. and three days of meetings and handshaking. Congress was in session and there were always too many questions about the base and the complaints of the neighbors.

Washington was its familiar self, the highway nicknamed the Beltway rolling through the green countryside to the government buildings.

At the Pentagon, Matthew signed in and threaded his way deeper into the mazes of hallways and offices. He found his commanding officer, Bill Murphy, in a prized outer ring office, and for two hours they went over Matthew's reports. As they moved to break for lunch, he asked casually, "Bill, what's the history on the base?"

"What kind?" came the answer, flat and guarded.

Matthew drew a breath. Usually his boss was hard to stop, full of the positives of base location and development, what benefits and jobs it brought people and areas.

"Well, the time since the '40s. There doesn't seem to have been much there before that."

"That's true." Nothing more. *In itself a statement,* Matthew thought.

They finished eating and strolled back to the Pentagon. Matthew saluted his goodbye, their immediate business complete.

Rule One: Don't let them know you are looking.

Matthew Rankin held that when you are straight-on in your course, steady in your turnings, others think they know what to expect from you.

Then unknown moments can be found that become yours alone. If you save up, hoard, gather these moments, slide them in where no one sees, then no one is the wiser and little things aren't noticed.

In the National Archives, some rooms, officially, do not exist. It is where much of America's past lies boxed and tabbed and quietly shelved. In an almost-hidden dusty alcove, Matthew found the legal cartons that held the history of the fleeting time America housed prisoners of the Second World War. Some military, much civilian, these camps dotted the country like a spiderweb laid flat.

He read dates, and found one marked with the time and base he was searching for: Camp Penn. Pulling it from the shelf above his head loosened a fine spray of dust onto his blue uniform. He looked around, but there were no places to read at leisure in these invisible rooms. No one did that here.

So the floor it would be, he decided, and slid down to sit with his back against more cartons, prepared to be there for a while. He undid the string wound around the keeper on the end of the box and pulled the flaps open.

Pay dirt, he said to himself. There were yellowed pages of base layouts and plans, a duty roster, and a rubber banded package of papers. He laid the items out in rows on the floor in front of him like a game of Solitaire.

Careful, crabbed handwriting noted everything. Soap and toilet paper and shampoo dispensed. Pants and shoes given out, kitchen supplies ordered, and what was used at each meal.

Another list kept track of the prisoners transferred in and out. There were many notes and crossed out lines on the pages, showing more movement in the later years. The groups seemed smaller and came and went more frequently, Matthew noticed. That fit with the ending of the war and the smaller camps, the satellite camps, that were being closed down, the men centralized and catalogued and shipped back to New York for a boat out to England. *They all went to England.*

The sun slid from one side of the small window to another, the bars throwing a grill of shadows across the floor and his legs as the afternoon waned.

At last, there was only the rubber-banded roll of papers left. Matthew picked it up and slid off the rubber band, unfolding the pages. It was actually a booklet, the front cover stamped in the middle, SOLDBUCH, in heavy black ink. Further down, the name Franz Becker ran across the page.

He turned to the next page and came to a straight-on, black-and-white photo of a man with light hair and eyes. Matthew studied it. Thirty years fell away in wrinkles and weight, and it was Jan. Just then his watch chimed softly, 1700 hours, day's end.

He slid the journals back into their dust-sleeves. Below, the buildings along M Street began to disgorge people onto the wide sidewalks.

Matthew watched the figures through the bars on the window, studying their purposefulness of their movements as they headed home. He gathered his jacket up and headed back up the street to the Pentagon, thinking as he walked.

He hadn't found anything about drums or barrels of anything except plane fuel. He entered the Pentagon and found Bill Murphy busy at the paperwork that meetings don't let you get to.

"Come in." Murphy waved a stack at him. "I've got to approve these supply requisitions for all the bases. They're running short on things we have to approve with this new budget central idea."

Matthew went to it straight and fast. *Surprise them with what you know.*

"Bill," he asked. "Did we practice chemical warfare on people?"

"No, Matthew, that's against the Geneva Conventions. You know that." Murphy tipped his head to look over his glasses at Matthew.

"Not even back in World War II?" he went on. "I thought perhaps with all the internment camps and prisoners of war, that we had tried it."

The challenge was out now, asking again when he had been gently shunted aside. The back of his neck tingled. Beware.

"Well, we didn't ever do that, for the record." Murphy's eyes tightened, just a bit, before he dropped his gaze and went on initialing.

Matthew watched him for a moment, silent. "How about not for the record, Bill?" he asked.

Murphy raised his eyes and looked at Matthew. "Not that I have personal knowledge of."

"But it might have happened."

"Damn it, Rankin, what is this?" Murphy slapped the folder onto the desktop. "We were at war. And it was a very long time ago."

"I know, just curious. I want to know what I live in the middle of."

Murphy sighed. "There was some incident up there. Drums of some chemical by-product were stored in tunnels, in a few of the extra rooms. At the time the tunnels were dug, we hadn't yet started to turn the tide on the war. So they planned the camps for half a million men, all spread out, so that the groups could not talk to each other."

He shrugged. "By the time Penn was built, the war had turned. We had won enough of France, and England was a surety, so that we began to put the prisoners there instead. We didn't need all the places here. So they were shut down and used for other things. Most of them are totally gone. You'll be lucky if you can find a building standing."

Murphy steepled his fingers and tapped them together.

"But you don't undig tunnels, so they were used for other things. And this stuff was corrosive, so they put the barrels down there. The barrels leaked, the chemicals ate the bottoms out of them, and got into the water. A couple of the prisoners developed some severe bleeding. At times, not always. Why, have you found something?"

His last words were short and clipped, a warning against more questions. Matthew shook his head, gut instinct telling him stop.

Drinks and steaks with the in-town group no longer sounded as inviting. The words Murphy had spoken, and those he clearly left unsaid, went round in his head and he could not get past them. Not tonight.

He caught a cab back to his hotel and had a restaurant dinner. The portions were small and dinner was over by seven o'clock. The evening stretched out ahead of him.

He changed clothes and went back to the National Archives to read the log. This time he wore civvies, brown pants and a plaid sport shirt, blending in with the throngs of people in the stacks and hallways and exhibits. This evening a guided display of America's Bicentennial was on the marquee, and the museum was crowded.

Several large groups waited patiently while their tour guides counted heads and bought tickets, noting things on a clipboard and shouting to marshal their groups into action, sending them one at a time through the turnstiles.

Matthew bought a ticket and smiled at the cashier, then made his way slowly again to the fourth floor. Up here there were no crowds.

He pulled down the box and again laid out the items, frowning as he tried to recall just how he had placed them that afternoon. At last he reached his leaving-off place and picked up the records of the prisoners.

He sifted through the pile of officer kept journals, looking for the final counting in the sequence. The right journal fell open in his hands, and he flipped through to find the last page with writing.

In the far right column was the same penciled total. 3003 in, 3002 out. He sat and looked for a minute, then went and copied those three pages on the floor below, the copier clunking before the pages shot out. The total was just visible, a shadow writing, rather than clear and legible. But there. Matthew leaned against the copier and studied the papers in his hand.

Was the missing number really raising cranberries just a few miles from where he walked away?

Matthew tucked his copies into a pocket and went back to put away the journals and cartons. He put them in date order, sliding the stack back into the carton. He collected his jacket from the back of the chair and melded into a group leaving, walking easily in their midst.

Most of them carried open-top shoulder bags and folders full of notes about what they had come to research. He kept his eyes on the middle distance, as though thinking of some vague and unhurried thing, and moved along in the flow. As though he were not aware of the blue uniform studying the faces of those exiting.

He had sensed his questions had bothered Murphy, and now he was sure. He walked on, the night air soft, not in a hurry to go back to his box of a room. He found a bench by the Potomac and sat watching the current slide down the middle of the wide water.

He was a soldier, this was his country, and things like this did not happen to him. The secrets he was charged with keeping were not his to decide about. His duty was to execute his orders, nothing more.

Why did he feel that this time it was different? Why did it matter if this time it was him who would make something he knew into something bigger, if he chose?

Around him, the city settled into evening's pace, the dim light softening the buildings and movement into a more gentle mode.

He found himself remembering the dim and cool Long Island attic of his childhood. The ceiling was hung with model planes built from fine bits of wood and silken wings and threads. They swayed gently in the breeze from the open door behind him.

Built by Robert, his older brother, one at a time, carefully and well, they had been Robert's escape, his refuge from their father's drunken rages; before he left, that was. But just yesterday, Robert had gone to war, and there was no longer any need for the planes or the refuge of the attic.

From below he heard quiet sobs and sighs. Robert had gone with his usual kiss in the sun-washed kitchen. Headed for class at St. Xavier's, where he was a senior. Supposedly. But he hadn't come home.

Just past his seventeenth birthday, now able to decide and act on his wish to fly for the Brits, Robert had gone to enlist.

"No, I won't hear of it," Mom had said more than once. "No. It's not your war and we need you here." And Robert, being Robert, hadn't argued. He didn't like conflict, or noise or pain.

"That's why I want to fly," he had told Matthew on a warm spring afternoon just a week earlier, his head bent over a tiny thread on a model of the Kittyhawk, the first Wright Brothers' plane.

"Up there, it is nothing but sun on clouds, and the world far below, tiny houses and ponds strung along the edge of the ocean."

Matthew had nodded. "But what if you crash?"

Robert answered him. "Flying, the world is so far away that you can't see the things that are wrong with it. All the uglinesses are too small to see, and all you have is one big, pretty place to look at while you're flying along. It's what I want to do."

So he had gone. Matthew thought that it was probably about the flying, but even more about the idea that the world was a bigger place than their Long Island house and Jones Beach and Saratoga in the summer. Robert had started to realize that. And, at last, he had bigger things to find and protect than Matthew and his mother.

But Matthew didn't have that; he was left with his mother and the sense of growing up all of a sudden that gets thrust on you by other people's expectations. When you become twelve and are suddenly the man of the house.

For three years they heard little, brief notes of places neither of them knew. Then on an afternoon of a soft fall day, Matthew had come home from school as usual and left his books in his room. The house greeted him with the kind of silence that says empty.

He waited all afternoon in the pale lemon sunshine, but no one ever came. At sunset he headed for the beach, just a mile from their house, and found his mother kneeling in the sand. She had come there often, more so lately, to walk restlessly and watch the waves. Other days, when Matthew asked her how she was, she would lay a quick hand along his cheek and say, "Fine, go home now." And she would walk some more. But this day he found her kneeling in the sand.

"I'm watching the water," she said.

"Why?" Matthew knelt beside her.

"Because this water, this ocean where we come to watch the sun, this water touches the other side." She looked at him.

"The other side of what, Mom?" he asked gently.

"That same water touches Europe," she said and put a finger into the surf. The water swirled around it, and small bubbles lay against the pinkness of her skin until the tide sighed out again.

She rose and made another pass along the beach, almost as if she were patrolling, pulling her sweater close against the breeze, seeking comfort and protection in the cold, clear air and tenuous bond of the water.

She held out the telegram then, brought to the house that noon by an officer offering respect and regrets. She came here to open it. Here, where she felt best.

"I was sure of the beach. I thought it was a magic circle," she told Matthew. "I thought he would come home if I wished it hard enough."

Matthew pried the telegram from her fingers. They were chilled and stiff and it took a long time, the way that things do when you know it will be bad and the minutes take forever.

We regret to inform you… Robert was dead, lost in a last-run mission. The date he died had occurred long before her beach desperation knew its reason. But, perhaps, it had been a part of her restlessness. Who can say what the heart knows and does not speak of?

And fifteen-year-old Matthew learned that day, that life did not always give choices and that a man did what he must do.

He stirred and looked at his watch, startled at the length of his reverie. Behind him a river of cars poured down the street. These things he had not thought of in so many years. *A man must do what he must do.*

The next morning he made his way back to the Archives one last time and took the carton from the shelf. He took Franz Beckers *soldbuch* from the carton, tucking it into his briefcase. He walked out once more into the morning sun and caught a cab for Dulles and his flight back to Boston.

Chapter 15

S ix weeks later, Matthew drove into New York and picked
Jan up. Graves had done a series of grueling chemotherapy
treatments, a stab at the high counts that signaled cancer.

Matthew walked into the hospital room and looked at the
old man sitting on the edge of the bed. In his mind's eye, he had
carried the younger Franz Becker and was startled now at the
aged one before him.

Jan looked back and nodded once, in greeting. "Okay, so
home I go?"

"How do you feel?" Matthew asked.

"Okay." Jan said.

Matthew reached into his pocket and held out the
soldbuch. "Your story was true. Do you want this?"

Jan considered. "No, I don't know that man anymore.
There is nothing left of him to look for. Nothing that I want to
find. It is better not to have it in my small place. What if someone
found it? Trouble would begin."

David Graves came in then and went over the chart with
Jan.

"Questions?" he asked. "Your counts point to cancer, but they're normal now."

"I have no other." Jan shook his head.

"Back to my patients then." He smiled slightly at Matthew. "The ones I really have. You'll be in touch if you need help?"

Jan told Graves, "I will take what comes." He stuck out his hand. "I thank you, Dr. Graves, for this chance."

The physician reached out and shook hands, his eyes not dropping from Jan's for a long moment. Then he flipped the chart closed and handed it to Matthew.

"Bring it back if you need to." He looked sharply at Matthew as they, too, shared a brief, hard shake. "One of the more interesting cases," he said. "What will you do with it?"

Matthew shrugged. "I don't know."

But he did. His mind hadn't changed since watching the Potomac's water.

The old station wagon threaded its way out of New York along the coast road. They wound down the windows when they got past Great Neck and drove out of the city amidst the evening exodus.

By the time they turned east at Wareham, they were seeing the cars from Boston, too, on Route 21. At last they swung east on the smaller road. The sea lay outside Jan's window, heavy with the smell of brine and washed up weed.

"Tide change," Jan said, and sounded pleased. He rolled the window down and rested his thin, white arm on the door and let the breeze blow full in his face for mile after mile. Night came on full and dark and by the time they crossed the Cape's bridge at Buzzard's Bay, the headlights shone bright on the heavy, pine forest pressing close along the sides of the road like walls.

The small clearing at Rachel's Corner appeared as the moon spun between dark clouds. Matthew pulled to a stop and turned off the engine. For a moment it was silent, and then the night-sounds began again, the ones Jan had heard for almost thirty years.

The sea frogs began their peeping and Jan said, "When I was getting the treatments, I kept that sound in my ears. It got me through some long days."

Matthew nodded. The neighboring bogman had left all in good order, it seemed. "Place looks okay," he remarked. Beyond the small house, the two horses watched intently from open half-doors on the stalls. Their eyes glowed red in the headlights. One of them nickered softly, but Matthew wasn't sure which one. It seemed a good night to come home.

"Yes," Jan said slowly, as if he had heard the words. "Thank you."

Matthew nodded. "You may get better now that the bleeding can be contained. What will you do?"

"Take the pills when I need them. It's harvest time. Lots of cold air and hard work. It's the only time I sleep well. Then I'm too tired for dreams."

He opened the car door and stood up. "I will try, anyway." He reached into his duffle and drew out a green, padded notebook and held it out to Matthew. "I wrote out for you my story," he said.

Matthew took the notebook and then the proffered hand. He drove away, the notebook lying on the seat beside him.

He wanted some pictures of the tunnels and drums. There was something dark in the denial Murphy had given him. Now, he swung the wagon into the old side road and drove slowly along its surface. The car swayed and dipped with the washed surface. The grade was smooth, tufted with some wild beach grass and washed some by the rain. But passable.

Matthew drove without headlights until the fallen tree came up on his right. Then he rolled to a quiet stop and loaded a roll of slide film into the camera. He stepped down into the tunnels and snapped pictures of the rusted old bits of barrels sitting in an oily, orange sludge, still there after thirty-plus years.

What, he wondered, *did we do in the name of protecting our country?*

In the clearing, lit by cold moonlight, all the trees were straight, bare-bleached trunks, and the ground was glazed with a dirty, hard film that broke into chunks when he dug his heel into it. Instead of the gritty, clean sand of Silver Beach, this soil coated and stuck to his fingers like oil paint gone bad. A dank, sour smell stayed on his hands.

He shot two rolls of film, thirty-six exposures each, and tucked them into a small canvas bag to be sent away for developing. But he still was not ready to go home. He started the car and rolled east again, until he came to a short road that went down to the beach.

He parked, doused the lights and listened to the waves roll in over and over against the sand. At length he got out of the car and moved through the trees to be nearer to the water. Jan Neuman's *soldbuch* rested stiff and bulky in his right front pocket. Now he took it out and sat, resting against an ancient piece of driftwood, looking at the book for a long time.

Then he rose and took the green binder from the front seat of the car and returned to his driftwood backrest. And in the light of the moon off page and water he found the rest of Jan Neuman's past.

What do you do when the path you followed does not go where you expected? When what you come to think is different from anything you might have imagined yourself ever thinking or feeling?

Matthew had believed, days ago, that he only wanted what he had always wanted, that a man should pay for what he did. Now he no longer knew. He held in his hands the material to chase Jan Neuman back to himself, back to Germany, back to face the awfulness of that war.

He opened his eyes and looked for stars, but a thin, milky cloud cover blocked his view. And he decided what Rule Number Four was: whatever you needed it to be. *Feel right.* He smiled to himself. Of all the rules he lived by, that one would be the only one that Manda might value. Maybe it was the best rule of all.

Dawn was a long time coming, and in that night he wished for three things. The first two were easy, a whiskey and a blanket against the ocean's chill. The last was not so comfortable a reach.

Somewhere in what he knew, part of what hadn't been said, were the secrets he might be held accountable for. His father had been a drinker, so wantful of a bottle that Matthew mostly avoided it.

But tonight he wanted to float far above these trees and beaches and ocean and a man he wished he didn't know. He raised the *soldbuch* and looked at the young Jan caught forever on its pages. The eyes gazing straight at the photographer, so that even now they seemed to watch, just a little.

This man, Jan Neuman. How had it gotten so complicated? How had Matthew gotten involved? He who stayed outside the messiness of life by staying within the bounds that rules set.

On the beach, with his back propped on damp driftwood and his clothes growing clammy with the sand, he wondered at what and where wrong began and ended.

That Robert had died? That Jan had fought this country? That long ago, men were housed and left near poisons? If you began the litany of awfulness, could you ever stop the count?

Did you begin with things of thirty years ago? The years since and what they had not done?

Was Jan yet one more soldier who had tried to serve his country, only to find it a place he did not know existed? He looked again at the man in the photo and sighed.

Matthew tucked the *soldbuch* into his briefcase and rose from his place damp with sand from knee to shoulder. He shifted the old station wagon into first and made his way along the dark road and back onto the base. He showered and changed at the office and called Ginny to say good morning.

While he was dialing, Matthew made his choice.

Chapter 16

Matthew was making his final check for the monthly National Guard drill weekend when he looked up and saw Phil Masters in his doorway.

"General." He rose and saluted.

"Rankin," two-star General Phil Masters said curtly and moved into the room. The blade-sharp creases on his khakis remained crisp even after he sat down. He placed his hands on his knees, looking around at the aerial photographs and activity charts hung on all the walls. Matthew had a working office.

Masters got right to the point of his visit.

"This is a good base, a viable location, but in this latest wave of peace signings, it has been targeted for deactivation."

The general nodded with each word, noting the importance of not being important anymore.

"This base?" Matthew stared at him. "After all the dollars we have put into it?"

"Yeah, things change," Masters replied briskly. "You'll return to either assignment mode within the Pentagon or to Texas, with our thanks for your service." He hesitated for a moment. "If I were you, I'd take the Texas route. Things at the

Pentagon may not be as comfortable for you. I've known you a long time, Rankin, since the Cuban Missile Crisis at Polk years ago. Brought your name up for this job.

"This business about chemical exposure - your questions have raised some interest that won't be easily put to rest."

Matthew Rankin watched him. "You mean I shouldn't have asked the questions?"

Masters sighed. "Some things are not to be asked."

"That isn't an answer." Matthew felt his shoulders tighten. He looked at Masters. "And that non-answer *is* an answer."

The general shifted. "Nothing on the record."

Matthew frowned. Masters took it as displeasure and leaned on the desk to make his point, stabbing his index finger down on the blotter that centered Matthew's workspace.

"There were decisions made that we only know bits of."

Matthew watched his general's star disappear in smoke over Masters' left shoulder. For a moment, he could swear that "Taps" echoed very faintly in the room. Once it would have bothered him, to know he would not make the next level. Now all he wanted was away.

Masters signed off on his duty papers and a driver took him to the runway to catch his flight to Washington. His last handshake to Matthew was hard and brief. The deal is done.

Matthew shuffled his papers together. Outside his door, the duty phone buzzed, answered by a voice he could not place. He looked at the clock above the door. Day's end - the night duty officer was on. He nodded agreement to Masters' words and had one thought. *They won't be looking for Jan. The quieter things are, the better.*

At home before dark for once, Matthew sat for awhile on the back steps of the house, the ones leading to the upstairs screened porch that looked out over the pond and the pines and the foxholes littered among the trees. Just months ago, he had sat here with Manda and listened to her story about the tunnels.

He rose from the stairs and went around the house to back the station wagon from the garage. He drove across the base swiftly and out through the Sandwich gate. The way to Rachel's Corner had become familiar. He knew which tree trunks to look for as the beams of his headlights swung across the pines closest to the road.

Still warm, the evening held an edge of chill, a faint taste of sharp and smokiness, the first hint that fall was sliding toward winter, that the green would soon flame into amber and then be drifted into snow.

He swung into the driveway and down around the turn to the house. He thought that it always seemed to be evening when he came. The horses' eyes gleamed an eerie yellow for a moment in the beams, then they turned back into their stalls to finish their hay.

From the small house, a curl of smoke added its acrid taste to the evening air. Matthew reached in the back seat and pulled out his flight jacket. Once the sun dropped, the temperature cooled quickly.

He crossed the yard and knocked on the door. Long moments passed before it opened, and he spent them drinking in the quiet of this place; just a small house set among trees edging the cranberry bogs to one side and a path to the beach on the other.

"Yes?" the door opened suddenly and yellow light spilled out, making Matthew squint and blink.

"Ah, is it all okay?" Jan asked, and motioned Matthew inside. Matthew took off his jacket, suddenly hot in the small room with the heavy smell of frying sausage in the air.

"I'm all right." He turned to face Jan. "I'm being transferred out. They are going to deactivate the base."

"Oh?" Jan watched him. In the skillet behind him, the sausage began to smoke.

"I don't think they know you are here," he went on.

Jan and moved at last to dump the burned pan of sausage out the back door. "You asked questions, then, about the tunnels? This is why?" He did not look at Matthew.

"Probably." Matthew said. "My boss, General Masters, was just here and seemed only to want me and my questions out of the way. I don't think they know you are here. If so, you are as safe as I can make you."

"So, to hide in plain sight, that's how I stay out of view?" Jan asked, and smiled a little at the irony.

"Yes, that's about the size of it." Matthew rose and reached into his pocket. "Since I won't be nearby anymore, do you want this now?" He held the *soldbuch* out to Jan, who looked at it thoughtfully.

"No, as I told you in the doctor's office, I do not feel that I know that man anymore. It belongs to someone who seems a stranger to me. Better not, I think."

Matthew returned the little book to his pocket and stuck out his hand. "I read your journal." His throat grew tight and hot. He had not meant to, but he had come to like the man he found in the pages.

"So this is it?" Jan asked. He had grown used to Matthew, pleased with the company after so much solitude. The visits had not been much or often, but they had been as much contact as he had for many a year. He reached out and took the hand offered him. Neither of them liked goodbyes.

****

Matthew went back to Texas, to run a base there until he retired with full honors. He cleared out his corner office that looked over the parade grounds that Custer had once trod, and put the last box in his car.

His silence had held well. It appeared that no one was aware of what he knew about prisoners who might have been kept near old barrels that leaked some unknown liquid. Liquid so caustic that it ate through heavy metal.

He had put it away. He and Ginny kept up with old friends, and some Air Force buddies came to Manda's wedding. He did enough other talking of other times and places that he did not stand out as oddly silent. He just did not speak of Cape Cod.

In Washington, ears stay to the ground. There are always people waiting to hear mutterings at comfortable backyard cookouts, intimate parties and gatherings, who immediately call on going home, passing along the old stories they had heard.

He put his secrets in an old footlocker and took it home with him, left to be found if someone cared to look. Where Manda might know what they were if she did.

He did not know of Pieter.

Chapter 17

Our House, Austin, July 20, 1996

The last sentences of Matthew's journal were cramped and tiny, two lines of writing squeezed into the space of one. I bent close to finish reading, then I turned the page and that was all, no more. The last date was October 16, 1975, not long before Matthew had brought us back to Texas.

My voice trailed off and I breathed deeply for the first time in what felt like hours. The clock on the wall read twelve thirty-two, so it had been hours. Around us night had fallen, our own black screen to play the journal's memories upon.

I ran my hand across the blank page, as though by touch I could make the rest of the story appear.

"And?" Pieter urged.

I shook my head. "There isn't any more." I closed the journal and sat for a moment.

We were part way to our fathers.

We all stared at the cover, so caught up in those long-ago words and the times they painted that now it felt unfinished to find only blankness beyond.

Next to me, Pieter reached past the journal and turned over the photo, looking at the writing on the back. Just a note and the date, May 1975. He tilted the picture and looked at it as though he could peek beneath its borders and see some other corner of the day it had been taken. But it lay flat and untelling in his hand, a celluloid image of two men together in a crowd.

A moment frozen and preserved. *Why?*

I reached then for the ragged, green book, Jan's words this time, to continue with our finding.

"Wait," Pieter said as I offered it to him. I did not read German. I faltered and waited, unsure. He had come so far, why would he not want to go on? The next scribing, after all, were words written by his father, and would contain more about his father than he had ever known.

But you don't know, always, what is in the heart or head of someone you are just learning.

Pieter sat for a moment, musing before he spoke.

"What about where it happened?"

"What do you mean?" I asked him, puzzled.

Pieter sat up suddenly and looked at us. "It is possible, no? I mean, in years it could be so, couldn't it? This sounds silly, I expect, ridiculous even, but do you think that this man that Matthew Rankin is writing about might still be alive?"

Cameron counted on his fingers. "He would be old now, almost eighty, but people do live that long or longer these days."

"Yes," said Pieter, "and so we better hurry."

"Hurry?" Cameron asked as he reached for his tea with lemon, sweat beading and sliding down the glass. I watched the droplets snake toward the bottom. I knew what was coming next.

"Yes, to this Cape, to this air base." Pieter looked at us. "To see if we can find this man."

Cameron and I glanced at each other. It did seem a thing to do. If my mother traveled in grief, so might I? Pieter thought this was about his father. It was, of course, but it was also about mine.

We sat for a moment and thought about the steps it had taken to get this far, to find what Matthew had left in different places, things that went together.

"I don't know," I said. "We know where he used to be, sort of, but not who to look for. Matthew never wrote about where exactly he left Jan. He never mentioned a place."

He had, only once, in all the pages of all the comings and goings, given a location. One margin held a doodle of a name, Rachel's Corner, in a faint scribble, as though a reminder to himself.

Writing probably as much for the release of putting on paper all those things that were secret for so long, but he had not slipped and told where this person could be found.

Matthew was, I knew, much wedded to the principles he held. And one of those bits of his code of honor was never betraying the things that he alone was charged with knowing.

I said as much, and Pieter agreed.

"Yes, I can see the soldier he was in the words he writes," he said. "I think he was serious about keeping faithful to the trust put in him. That was obviously important from the way he has written these pages."

"It's possible, I guess," said Cameron, "to find this Jan." He shrugged.

Pieter edged forward and asked, "What about going to where you lived when the picture was taken?"

"We only know the location of the one from New York," I pointed out. I thought about all the slides, "We don't know where the other shots were taken."

"We won't know if we don't look," Pieter said.

Cameron turned to me. *It's not for me to say*, his eyes said. *Go or not*.

I want to look, my own replied.

Silently he agreed, *OK then*.

Just then Pieter spoke and both Cameron and I jumped, suddenly remembering that he was there. "I think I do not want to know more of this story just now, not until I find out if this man, this Jan, might be alive." He looked down at his hands. "But I know you may want to go on and read this other book."

He handed me the open *soldbuch*.

I thought about it and carefully closed the cover, smoothing my hand across the frayed fabric. I had read about my father doing something he did not have to do, and it felt enormously more than I had known before, and for this minute I was content.

Still, I would want to know, want to meet if I could, the man who so held Matthew's loyalty.

We all nodded at once, like the three Musketeers.

"I guess I get to see Cape Cod," Cameron said.

"I guess you do," I agreed.

"I haven't ever been there," he said to Pieter.

"Nor I," said Pieter with a smile.

I thought that Cameron would like the Cape, at least the one that I remembered, but Pieter would probably not see anything beyond a blur of sea and pines, his mind fast-forwarding toward the man he might find there.

Only then would all this have perspective for him. Until then it was only a hole. One he needed to fill.

Pieter left at one in the morning, his car door and engine loud in that hour's silence. I sipped the last of the coffee and tried to summon the spirit of Matthew, not just the facts and stories, but who my father was.

Shortly after we went to bed, still silent, and as I closed my eyes, I made my mind a canvas to be filled with memory's brushstrokes. But they wouldn't come.

I must have slept at last, for I dreamt of Matthew. Of burying him when the planes flew over the cemetery and the chaplain spoke of "going home" under the wing shadows. I carried his words away with the petals of the roses each mourner moved to lay on the grave.

And Matthew stood behind a tree two headstones away and kept an eye on me. No one seemed to notice him. They went on staring fixedly at the grave. He stood looking at no one but me.

Cameron woke me as he left to start his day. My neck was stiff, my mouth dry and cottony.

"Okay?" he asked me.

"Yes." I was already starting a list in my mind of what to pack for the journey. First on the list was the green book, words to travel unread in my dark suitcase, curiosity going along for the ride.

Three hours later, I sat next to the travel agent's desk in the American Express office near our house.

"Need insurance?" she asked brightly.

"No, just the tickets." I answered her.

The agent pushed a button, giving me a total for the tickets. I made a mental note that advance travel is much cheaper.

I signed the credit card receipt she laid in front of me, feeling a bit like 007. Two days later we boarded a flight to Boston with the unread book riding in my carry-on bag.

Chapter 18

Early September 1996

L ike a finger crooked in beckoning, Cape Cod lies eastward of the Massachusetts mainland, curving north into the sea just below where the second knuckle might be. *Come, it says, cross my bridges to a small and charmed and isolated world apart from the grubbiness of city living.* The Kennedys made it famous for sailing and seafood and football with the ocean for an audience.

At the fold of the bottom knuckle, tucked in the skin crease where a seer might find a lifeline, lay the place I lived between thirteen and sixteen.

****

They say you cannot go back again, not home, not really. And that's true. You cannot undo time gone by.

We are a sum total of our experiences at any clock-strike in our life. Hindsight's lucidity is a danger, in that it distills and clarifies the happenings of then into the results of now.

In recalling, it is easy to forget what you did not know then, at the time you made the choices that you have come to question later.

And there is the peril that no matter how many words you speak, or the length of the silences when you don't, it is impossible to bring someone else to a full understanding of your own memory, both what you remember and what you don't. You can only show what is and try to recreate what once was for your listeners.

****

The hopper flight from Boston to Hyannis skimmed roads and trees and shoreline. I had forgotten the breathlessness of small plane flying. I sat pressed against the window the whole time, drinking in the view.

Below, a scattering of familiar landmarks helped me orient myself. The twin bridges came into view over the canal. One of the bridges was raised, and a ship moved slowly through the channel that cuts across from Cape Cod Bay to the ocean around Nantucket. A thin ribbon of white sand edged the blue water between sea and the green darkness of trees.

When you are among them, the trees close thick about you, and you feel like an adventurer exploring new lands. I recalled riding Skye along on a firebreak or narrow road and then rounding a curve to find a village tucked away against the trees.

I never did like landings and didn't that day either, when we slipped lower and lower toward the Hyannis airport. But our pilot touched us down deftly and we climbed from the plane, crossing the tarmac to the walk-in terminal. I stopped for a moment, breathing in the tang of pine and ocean mingled in the warm afternoon air.

Our car was ready. We tucked the bags into the trunk and headed to Falmouth, to a B&B where I had booked two rooms. Cameron drove slowly, watching. Pieter stared out of the windows.

"It is something like home, the blueness of the water," Pieter said. "And the pine trees."

Memory stirred. Our ocean in Texas was not like this - the water is flat and gray and the beaches are tan. It doesn't have the vividness, the blue-green spectrum these waters hold, nor the sheer, empty beauty of this sand beside the surf.

We drove along roads that were both familiar and not. The routes were the same, but much else was different. There were many more houses than before, neat and small Cape Cod cottages with simple walls of cedar-shake siding and steep rooflines.

The next morning, I leaned on the railing of our balcony and watched the ocean below, steel blue in the early light. Behind me in the room were the sounds of Cameron dressing.

Some people may study themselves in the mirror when toweling off, pink and naked and wavery-imaged in the steamed glass. Then as the mirror clears and the reflection grows sharper they hurry to dress, to cover the truth of themselves and keep it from the world and their own eyes.

Cameron is not one of those. He is slim-hipped and lanky, naked or in blue jeans. His steps are the same, unaltered, wherever he goes and have been since I met him. I heard his footsteps grow louder; the curtain parted and he slid behind me, circling me in his arms. I leaned against him and smelled the fresh scent of soap and shampoo and the spice of his aftershave.

I had been leaning on Cameron for a lot of years as friend and lover and mother and wife.

Earlier, we had gone for a walk down the beach just as the sun was first limning the horizon. At that moment the ocean was perfectly still, a deep purplish mirror with a hint of light behind it. It was Cameron's first time to watch and walk and observe the quietness of Cape people, the beach-combers and ocean-watchers who chose the edgings of a day to pay homage to its coming.

From over the water came the growl of trawlers, just clearing the far edge of the bay, faint shapes with lines and towers and swooping groups of birds following in their path.

At home we didn't have dawn and ocean like they did here. Nor the expanses of marsh grass and sand-drifts and the immense sense of aloneness that these Cape Cod beaches bring.

In my teenage summers here we learned quickly to go to town early, then to stay near our own ponds and trails during the daytime rush of people. Back then, the Cape had only one road and a single accident could leave you sitting for hours along the paved lanes.

Now it was bigger. A new bridge, a new piece of highway, houses and restaurants and business, all quaint and tucked within their own little spaces so that at first you did not notice that the space was much taken up with all of them, backed as they were by the empty stretches of sea. Perhaps you only saw it if you were here before and had known the silent stretches of woods and sand and water.

Among those places, were we going to find Jan Neuman? Or Franz Becker?

"It's nice here," Cameron said. Today the breeze brought us a hint of salt water and pine, coming from the north, where the chill air kept the scents fresh for us.

I kept looking for things to be the way I had known them. Some of them were there; the diner where we ate meatball subs, and the tiny Sears pickup store in Falmouth where Ginny had ordered my first makeup.

I had first curled my hair here, only to watch it fall from the ocean's dampness, and I had my first kiss here, hot enough to make my mascara stick and clump, sitting in the front seat of a tiny MG, watching this same ocean.

I flashed on the memory of keeping my eyes seductively closed, as sixteen imagined, so that my date would not know my eyelashes were stuck almost shut from hormones and steam and humidity.

I learned to wear waterproof mascara, to kiss more slowly, because fire's kindling needs a careful, thoughtful touch.

I brought my thoughts back with a smile. Today we would drive and look and try to find that next link that might connect Pieter to his father. I needed to go and get ready.

Chapter 19

Pieter

In his room, Pieter also was getting ready. He had dreamt a familiar dream the night before. When he began to shave at sixteen, he wondered how his father's beard had grown. Like other boys, he had been proud of the sprouting, the signs of manhood within himself.

But other boys had a father to teach them how to use a razor, how to keep the sharpness from scraping away too much skin. You did not want, he learned, skin exposed to the world and the air as a red, weeping scrape of the tender flesh, showing you were just learning the first tough lessons of manhood.

Even more than razor lessons, Pieter missed seeing how his father's beard grew. How often had he needed to shave? Daily, weekly, twice a day? Ought he wear a mustache, a goatee? The whiskery unkempt look that was a sign of unGermanness in 1991? Was his own, Pieter's beard, anything like his father's? Or maybe someone else? He did not know; his mother's answers were vague.

"I don't know, Pieter. He shaved. He was always shaved close and smooth, except for when he had just come back from a training. But I do not remember how often he shaved. Just that he did."

Slowly he grew to realize that Eve's memories were isolated, still shots, a moment, an image of a person, but not depicting the breathing and living they had done. He had an image of his father, a view of what he had looked like, but still no sense of how or why he looked at the world as he did.

****

Manda

The sun was up a good bit by the time Pieter knocked on our door and joined us on the balcony.

"Good morning," he said, and I heard anew his English flavored with crisp exact words, each one pronounced completely and just so. I was more used to the drawl of the South, or the twang of Texas people. We made two syllables wherever we were able.

Matthew always said that he thought Texans stretched the words out because they were too hot to finish them with any energy. They just sort of left off speaking on any breath of air, and sooner or later they'd run down. Or they just cut the letters off and let the listener fill in what was missing.

We gathered the last of rolls and coffee that were the Continental breakfast included with our rooms, and headed for the car. I watched Pieter move ahead of me. He walked quietly, but in his shoulders was a stiffness I had not seen before. I glanced at Cameron, who nodded back. We would let our guest choose.

I asked Pieter, "Which way first?"

"*Ach*, I do not know." Pieter looked in both directions.

It was strange, but this part didn't worry me. I guess I thought that if I could find the place, the answer would be there, like a shell on the sand. And that if I looked at something I had found, somehow that would be an answer about what Matthew had known or done or not.

"I don't know how to go about looking for someone who doesn't want to be found," I said.

Cameron leaned against the car roof. "Me neither," he said, "but we have one big advantage."

Pieter and I waited, and Cameron went on to say, "Whoever he is, he probably doesn't know we are looking. I would think that if silence has worked for so long he may be easy about it. He may not think he has to hide."

Pieter nodded. "It is not as though anyone wants to get him in trouble." He looked at me. I did not know what to say. I had not thought beyond what I would do once I knew the facts.

For many a year, people have come to Cape Cod to get away, drawn to summer removed from the outer, mainland world. And for centuries, and even longer, women have waited for their men to sail back into this bay and the harbors that dot its curves.

Houses here are old and solid, built of pine and sometimes rock, set deep and sturdy to withstand the gale winds that occasionally blow, the still, white silence of snows and the quiet of men who do not come home.

I could imagine walking up the stairs to stand on the widow's walk and watching the bluish-hazed line of the horizon. Looking for the solid line of a mast that would signal a ship's approaching.

The cemeteries here were old as well. Headstones tell of a different time and way of dying. The Sandwich cemetery lies between a church and a pond with an old gristmill along its edge. Those sleeping forever have a view of blue water and white ducks in the sunshine. Some graves are tiny, the resting places of the many children who did not survive.

Everywhere there are signs of life having been lived for a long time.

"Where now?" Cameron asked, beside me.

I was not sure. Pieter shrugged, open palms up, no starting point in mind.

So we began with where I had lived. The former Air Force base lay open now, part of it a military cemetery and part of it a national park. We crossed onto the main road and followed signs to the airfield.

When I had lived there, pilots and planes had come and gone at all hours. The Navy had many families there as well. Personnel for the cutters they kept at Woods Hole, home to oceanography studies and rescue missions.

Now it was silent. A few of the buildings I remembered were still there. Small, neat plaques gave each building's name and smaller print offered a paragraph about their function.

It was a museum now, a life-sized relic. But it was not home, and nothing spoke. We drove back out past the snapping flags to the rotary with roads spiking off in all directions. We circled twice.

"The tunnels are that way," I pointed to the left. Cameron took the turn and we drove down a narrow, paved road, back and forth. The only thing in sight was a heavy, tall chain link fence with large "Do Not Enter" signs hanging from it.

"I think that fence is about where we want to be," I said at last.

Cameron pulled off the road and we walked to the fence. The chainlink had a matting on the backside, too, making seeing inside difficult. I found a rock to stand on and peered through the narrow gap between the chainlink and the top pipe frame. Beyond it, I could make out the dark opening of the tunnel entrance.

"That's it, we're here," I told them excitedly. "They've got it blocked off."

We walked the fence line a bit more, but it ran tall and strong as far into the trees as we could see. We would not get close to the tunnels, not today, anyway. We got back in the car and went on out the Sandwich gate.

What next?

We stopped and spread the map across the hood of the car, the fresh creases stiff and stubborn to unfold, so that it caught in the wind and blew up into our faces until Pieter placed his hands across two corners to hold it down.

I traced my finger along the jagged line of coast, up, along and back again to the wider part of the green.

I said, "Oh." My fingertip sat gently next to a half-dollar cove just beyond the Sandwich Woods.

"Rachel's Corner" was there in faint, pink letters. The same as written on the back of the picture of the cottage by the sea.

We were not careful refolding the map. Cameron started then engine, and Pieter sat forward in his seat. I wondered, not for the first time; what if Jan were dead?

****

How odd it must seem at fifty-six to be looking for your father.

How odd it was to be a part of it, the catalyst for someone's looking. I wondered now as Cameron checked his watch and looked at the sun's angle, *how much did this man that we sought know? Anything? Nothing? If we found him, would he want to be found? How easy would it be on the strength of a picture, a stranger's word and a child's recall of footsteps to prove he was the man Pieter wanted to remember? No, I told myself, that last part is not right.*

It is not as much who Pieter wanted to remember as it was whom Pieter wanted to remember him.

In a clearing along the Sandwich Road, a small sign had been pounded into the sandy ground: "Rachel's Corner". We drove and walked and visited. And found nothing at first.

"How about something to drink?" Cameron asked, pulling off onto the sandy shoulder of the road.

Just beyond it was a silver-shingled vendor's stand with large wooden doors propped up to form a covered buying area. Wooden trays held blueberries and cheeses and breads and jars of jellies that glowed in the sunlight.

A figure moved in the back; a man behind the counter was busy at straightening up and wiping from one end to the other. As he turned, the bulk of his shoulder caught my eye.

Something in the tilt of the head reminded me of someone just beyond the edge of memory.

I walked in front of him, and he turned full round. Blue, blue eyes took my measure. I looked right back and could only think that in a black-and-white picture, blue is only one more shade of gray.

But Pieter's eyes were not a photo.

I reached out and gripped Cameron's arm. His eyes followed the slant of my gaze.

"Let's get that drink," he said and moved toward the counter. I followed, Pieter just behind. This was almost out of our hands now, we were just messengers, intermediaries, footmen, passing on something that began before us, something whose end was really for someone else to make.

I moved toward packages of spiced pumpkin bread mix, and Cameron stooped to pull drinks from a wooden crate of iced bottles on the floor.

Pieter moved to the counter, into the smoky smell of cheeses and their waxed wheels glowing amber in the dim light against the fresh wood shavings they rested on. Cameron and I watched. Pieter looked around and selected a small wheel of Vermont cheddar, hefting it in his hand.

"For us," he said, and moved toward the man.

"Can I help you?" The old man glanced up.

Pieter went still, so still that even his breathing was impossibly loud. I knew he had studied that picture so long and often that the shape of the man's head was imprinted on his mind's eye. And now, before him, like the last piece of a jigsaw puzzle, the angle and curve fit exactly. All of a sudden, it was there.

****

How do you go about asking someone who they are? When you already think you know who they have been and are not anymore? I think, in our mind's eye, somehow we thought to find a young and virile Nazi captain working and sweating. One not aged by the passing of years or the weight of his own doings. I did not know the details of how and why this man had stayed, but it must have been striking enough to catch and hold Matthew's feeling of importance.

I did not think after all this searching, that it would be hard to start a conversation. But it was.

Pieter stood motionless, hands in his pockets, the cheese forgotten on the counter, watching cars going by on the road out front. Cameron kept sorting fruit and glancing over at me. I watched the old man, trying to see in the wrinkles and sun-burnt tan the man from years before. I think I must have been hoping as much for Matthew in his face as for Pieter's father.

In these days, when suddenly I could no longer ask Matthew himself, I kept longing for some sense of connection in these places he had been.

We were the last customers and were obviously no longer buying, yet also not leaving.

At last he said, "Is there something else I can get you?"

I took a deep breath and looked hard at Pieter, thinking, *this is the moment you came for.* He had come half a world to see if his father lived, and now standing right in front of him, seeing him in the flesh, Pieter did not have a word to say.

He kept staring fixedly at the trees, the sandy ground and coming night. Cameron quirked an eyebrow at me as if to say, he *must do this.* The quirk becomes a frown I studiedly did not see, all my attention of choosing as carefully as I could. *You cannot do this for him.*

I almost turned to go, and then stopped. *I wanted the answer.* Pieter might not, after all, but I did. I had found more in the pages of my father's writing than I had ever known before, and I wanted to know what came next. Somehow I knew that the end of the journal wasn't really a blank page. So maybe the urging had to come from me. I wanted to know what this man might know about my father.

I drew a deep breath and said, "I am looking for someone - maybe you can give me directions." Behind me, Cameron's glare took on a laser-beam intensity that I could feel hot on my shoulder-blades.

"I will if I am able," The old man waited.

A car swerved in just then and a quartet of plaid-shorted tourists noisily compared and chose. They paid and moved out to their car, talking and counting change as they went, one of them waving a map in the air.

I had dug in my backpack while waiting and found the picture, the one of Matthew and the man, Franz Becker, caught in the melee of Grand Central Station. I held it out and he took it casually, then he did not move for a long moment. Cameron and Pieter both stood, watching me as if they could not believe what I was doing.

I think a younger photo might have been hard to match, but Jan had been fifty when that picture was taken, and age has a look all its own, settled and boned - as we have by then become who we were ever meant to be.

"Where did you get this?" he asked me. He glared at me, with the blue eyes Pieter had, only deeper.

"I came across it in some photos someone took a long time ago," I said.

"I know who took it," he interrupted me. "What I want to know is how did you get it? Where is the man who did the shooting?"

Pieter moved, then, finally.

"I was given it by a man named Prang," he said. "I went to a battalion reunion in Germany for units in the war."

In front of me the old man grew still, so that I did not even see him breathing for a moment, but his eyes watched.

"How is it you went to the reunion?"

"I went to find out about my father's unit."

"And this man, this Prang?"

"He told me that he saw my father long after the war. In New York City, in 1975, when he took this picture."

"What is your name?" The old man's voice had gone high, as though someone had punched him hard in the stomach. As though he could not get his breath.

Pieter reached into his pocket, and brought out something in his cupped hand, opening it gently. An object rolled and rattled on top of the glass case, and I moved closer to see a tiny horse lying in the light. It was brought from a cold and distant place, by a young father who missed his son. But I did not know that then.

The old man stood for a long time staring down at the horse.

At last he looked back up at Pieter, "Again, your name?" he asked, his voice grated, guttural and harsh, as if it came from a place long not touched.

"Pieter," said Pieter. "My name is Pieter Becker."

"Gott in Himmel," said the old man.

And a father and son took measure of each other across a lifetime of not known years.

****

Pieter tried to say Papa but his throat closed up tight. Bile rose in a bitter surge, and he fought a wave of nerves. He closed his eyes, willing the nausea away.

It worked. The world quit swaying under his feet, and his ears stopped ringing. When he opened his eyes, dark and light no longer fought for space or licked along the edges like the flames of a fire. He swallowed and tried again.

"I think you are my father." His own voice sounded in his ears, more steady and clear than he had hoped for.

"I expect I am," the old man replied, his eyes very blue upon Pieter. They stared, unmoving, at each other, and the silence stretched out between them like a rope pulled tight between two trees.

Pieter pondered, trying to break the silence into small enough chunks that it could be carried. Or would fifty years become sixty, of unsaid regret and silence?

"I have searched a long way for you," Pieter said at last, trying to bridge the gap between a life of not knowing this man and the immediate fact of finding him here in this place, between the small pines and the sea.

"I lived a long time here," Jan answered "I call myself now Jan Neuman."

"After all this time is there no more to say than that?" Pieter asked.

Jan considered. He did not, had not, spoken often through the years, and never quickly. Except with the horses, he kept his secrets. Into those swiveled ears he spoke freely.

But things of the heart were harder, especially when there is both love and hate bound up in the same threads of memory, woven into the same cloth of time.

"No, it is not all there is to say or not say. It is that I am not sure of what to say." Jan stared at Pieter.

His son. That one thing that most men want, something to leave their mark upon the world. The question is whether that mark is a smudge or a flourish.

Jan roused himself to bring down the panels and lock them carefully into place.

"Come," he said. "We are needing to talk, I think."

We followed Jan down a sandy lane, winding through some trees to a cottage by the sea. As we parked, I had a flash, a sense of Matthew. I had come to a place where he had been.

If I turned fast enough, would I see him?

No, but I felt nearness to him there.

Inside I unzipped my backpack and placed the green book upon the table.

"Ah, so long ago," said this old man and cupped a hand on either side of it, as if through cradling those days might make them come again.

He sighed and appeared for a moment even older than his years.

"I must tell you who I am now," he said. "And who I was, once upon a time."

And so we settled in to listen. Outside, the darkness lay like a curtain on the world.

Chapter 20

Jan/Franz, Cape Cod, Summer 1996

T here is no one story of World War II that really tells it all. Some tales seem untrue, and others speak of courage and sacrifice and trying. All a man, Jan, could offer were his own tales, colored by time. He had not talked or thought about them in a very long time. That, perhaps, made them more true to themselves than the ones that are discussed and retold. For all of us recount things a bit the way we wish them to be, and our memories change in the telling.

Jan no longer thought of the war in the terms of countries and what they wanted, either for themselves or those they rolled across. He thought of the people, the little lives that were ground up or changed or ended in the machine of world events. He did not know anymore if he was a man of the world, not this one anyway. But that was by choice.

Remembering, Sometime in the 1940s

In Germany, the one he grew up in and thought he knew, people clung much to the past. He thought perhaps that was because times more current shamed them.

He had had a lot of time to think in all these years. Much was expected of a first son in Germany. It was almost as much a foundation of the country as the massive blocks of gray rock that made up so many of the buildings there.

And the stones that paved and lined the streets. He remembered that even on a sunny day, Berlin seemed gray. Unless the sun was full and clear - then it washed the gray into softness and you noticed more the splashes of color against the sameness of all that stone.

The people who built this country did so with lastingness in mind. They planned and thought and undertook so that these edifices, these monuments, would last for more than one generation. They believed in the passing on of their heritage and built to show others the depth and superiority of their thinking.

The dark hulks of those buildings remained. Once they housed and held power and might and ideas that bore a people far away from themselves. Later, gutted and bombed and ruined, they were what would be remembered.

He was born as Franz Becker, the first son of a banker in Elenruhe. His childhood was spent in more than comfortable circumstances. There was money enough for meat and fresh vegetables year round, good clothes for Sunday, the opera in Berlin, even yearly trips to France or Spain.

He loved to go to Berlin by train. Every few months they would board at sunset from the Elenruhe station. The coaches had leather seats and curtains against the dark, and inside the crystal lamps glowed soft and yellow. They traveled in a warm, small world of their own, rocking through the night until they came to Berlin and stepped down into a bustling, dark world where no one ever seemed to sleep. He remembered most the tiny, white lights that traced the doorway of the hotel where they always stayed.

The twenties and thirties were a rich time for Germans, the ones that he knew. So many music and books and plays were written and performed and applauded.

German engineering and doctors made discoveries and inventions that astonished the world. He recalled his parents dressing for the opera; remember mostly how sweet his mother smelled, and how tall his father seemed in a tux with tails. He did not recall the times in Germany before this.

He was born in 1918, just after the Armistice was signed. By the time he was old enough to remember, the proof positive of that conflict had washed away. He was at the age, teens and twenties, that all the possibility and glitter that seemed so alive in Berlin made a deep impression upon him. There did not seem to be anything Germans were not masters of.

Perhaps that is where the thinking started, the thought that there should be masters of all places, times and people.

At home, he went to a good school where the masters were strict about learning. And he learned well. After school, there was a boys' group, and one for girls. This group was not a choice. If you went to the school, you belonged. But he did not mind. The groups spent time learning why Germany had so many talents to offer. And they were told what other countries and people did not do to celebrate their opportunities. When he was sixteen, he graduated and was ready for college.

There was a restlessness in his homeland that year that matched one within himself that would wake him in the night. Things were changing, people were going without jobs and money, and a new leader was promising much to anyone who would listen. His name was Hitler.

During those times, rumors whisperings began, also, of villages and towns and distant places that Germany was moving into. But he did not listen much to the details as Germany began to expand its borders, not even when several friends left college and went into the military.

This was a highly applauded and encouraged course of action within their group. It was putting your country's needs ahead of your own, honoring the Fatherland.

Those from his group who had gone to serve came back with stories of the extreme poverty in countries, such as Poland. They said these places needed to become a part of Germany; they needed someone to lead them, to free them from their own ignorance and inability to move forward.

He wanted to see some of these countries and friends, and he signed up after an emotional and deep-felt speech by a classmate, Gunter, who had recently returned to university after a two-year stint.

Gunter had moved back into the dorm with Franz and the other boys and taken up his classes again. Franz would find him staring at the river rather than reading, and he was restless.

Then, on a fall afternoon when they were all sitting in the warm sun drinking beer, he began to speak about Poland. Green fields which were empty of crops and animals, and cities full of people who needed help. The Polish did not know what was good for them, he said. And he made Franz see the poverty and the need. And he wanted to help Germany in this effort to bring others up to a good life. And so he went.

Looking back, Franz did not remember fear, though the events of the day were clear to him. He went and took his physical. The doctor poked and prodded. It was funny the way you remember moments, like when the doctor put the stethoscope between his shoulder blades. The chill had gone so deep he could swear he felt it touch his heart.

Later, he realized he'd only felt that chill two other times in his life. As he walked out of the prison camp and as he watched the bombing of a village.

Franz passed the physical and was encouraged to volunteer for duty on the eastern edge of Germany's efforts. No one called it the front then; that was an American word that appeared to be when the German effort became a living, breathing, definable thing.

He decided to do as he was asked, but leaving was a hard thing. His place in the business had been set. He was to take over from his father and this absence would be difficult for the others who worked there. It was decided that his brother, Hans, the youngest of the five offspring, would assume Franz's role so he could go.

Around him, he saw speeches and pamphlets that spoke of the great sense of duty to society, a duty to help Germany keep expanding its culture and discoveries. He was to serve for the next two years.

The hardest part of that was Eve. Since he had first seen her in the stirrings of early womanhood, they had eyes for each other. And more. They had spent a number of warm, still afternoons on a blanket in the thick pines that ring the Blausee.

On the last day, their kisses grew hot and slow, and the sky and trees melded with what they did that day. After, Eve rested with her head on his shoulder.

"What are you thinking?" she asked.

"Nothing," he answered, but he was. He was thinking that this was the first time he had felt emotion stronger than reason. He would have done anything to bed Eve that day.

They did not speak, but dressed at last and went home in the evening. It had been expected that they would marry upon his finishing his studies that year.

The next week splintered his world, when the Nazi war machine made immediate service mandatory. For a few weeks he lived in two pieces. Eve and her mother were already picking linens and silver to store in a heavy cedar chest that took up a great corner of her bedroom.

In three days' time he must report to the camp, for transportation there would be a troop train.

The families went into motion and Eve and Franz married at noon two days later, at the city manager's office, with only his brother as an attendant and both sets of parents as witnesses.

They hurried back to the small flat so he could pack his shaving kit and clothes and grab his soldier's papers, his *soldbuch*, which listed his training, where he was from and what he was assigned to do. They had one night alone and then he was standing in line to board the troop cars at the Elenruhe station.

He remembered the tears in Eve's eyes. As she let go of his hand, her eyes pooled and filled until they swam like a lake in full sun. Each tear made a dark blotch on her green dress as they fell, one at a time, oh, so slowly.

The train pulled away and he stood on the metal stairs and watched Eve get smaller in the distance until a sergeant ordered him inside.

When he looked back later, he was unsure how he so quickly went from being a man just done with marriage vows and bed, into being a soldier with little on his mind but the taking of towns and lives. But that is what happened. Within two months, he received notice twice for his zeal and efforts in the name and honor of Germany. When the vote happened to cede power to the Reichstag, he did not remember having any doubts. And he got word that Eve was with child. A son was hoped for.

He was sent to France, to help keep the occupation of France not only calm, but productive.

Franz grew to think the French were a volatile, voluble people whom could never quite be counted on when he was not watching. In the south of France, the Germans repeatedly lost and retook any number of villages and roads that kept their route to the coast and train lines open.

Again, he was given commendations for the job his platoon did in taking an assigned mark or defending a position that had come back under attack by the French.

The French people were of several minds; some were openly welcoming and wanted to join Franz and his troops. Others were quiet, but did as they were told to do. Some were openly hostile and resistant to German presence.

The German military deemed that houses and farms were to be at army disposal. The families were packed off with what they could get into one small wagon, and they were allowed one horse or animal to pull it. Franz moved into billet in an old stone farmhouse set in a field outside a town called Alencon.

Franz remembered that in the room that he was assigned, he found a small set of pearls, well-matched in size and carefully tucked away.

He had been given a girl's room, and he tossed the pearls to the corner, impatient with prettiness. Somehow they broke, and tiny beads bounced and clattered across the wooden floor. He did not mean for them to break, and thought then for a moment of the child whose room this had been.

He noticed them, perhaps, because word had been sent that Eve had been safely delivered of a boy. But he was celebrating fatherhood, and did not think of the pearls again.

Eve and their son were living in the second-floor flat she had taken just as they were married. It was across the main street from the train station, and it had a corner balcony twice as wide as the other apartments in the building.

Eve named the boy Pieter and reported that he loved, even at three months old, to watch the smoke and steam from the trains as they came to the station each day. She also wrote that the furniture had come at last, and she was trying to arrange their new home around Pieter's schedule.

Because the balcony was so long, two rooms opened onto it with French doors and long windows that gave the rooms a lot of light.

Eve wrote that the families had been generous, giving them many pieces of furniture. But it was all large, and she was trying to fit it into the two rooms' space. And so she put the heavy dining table in the corner of the living room between the French doors on one wall and the kitchen door on the other. It rounded out into the room but she just moved around it. It had belonged to Eve's grandmother. Eve wrote that she kept the chairs against the wall for the sake of space.

When Pieter learned to walk he could pull himself up and edge from the kitchen to the balcony, going from chair to chair.

On the balcony, Eve kept some small potted roses and blooming plants. Pieter would scoot himself out there and dig in the dirt of the pots. Finally Eve gave in and had a square, wooden tub full of dirt put in for him to play in. He seemed, she wrote, to like feeling things grow. She thought that was because of the farmers in their families.

Franz thought it might have been because the child was conceived on a blanket by the Blausee.

But that was not to be written in letters that were censored. And it would not have been a thing for the families to know.

Then, from their place on the edge of the German effort, soldiers began to hear rumors that their unit, that many of those in the area, were going to be pulled off and sent somewhere else. Franz' skills as an artillery captain were growing in importance because the balance of the war was changing. The Eastern Front was said to be struggling.

Again, on a day's notice, Franz was ordered there.

This train was much different than those he had taken before. The cars were much older and broken, with no heat and not enough seats for the men they carried. Franz listened to the talk around him as they rocked over the uneven tracks. It was too cold to sleep.

The supply lines were faulty, being interrupted or completely disabled along their lengths. It was being said, passed among the troops in whispers, that the German effort was spread very, very thin.

The Eastern front was never completely stable. The distance from Germany to the fighting in Russia was a problem. Not just in the way of supplies, but in the feeling of comradeship to one's country and position. Russia was fiercely cold, and Franz stepped off the train into a blinding, raw snowstorm. The flurries would swirl in a matter of moments and obliterate all that could be seen just seconds before. Soon a man came by, tying a thin rope from one man to the next.

Franz waved him away, "Stop, what are you about?"

The man went on tying Franz's knot. "You will need it. You cannot see in front of you when the wind stirs the snow in circles. You are tied so that you do not veer off into the trees alone and freeze to death. Such a thing has happened many times." The man gave the knot a last yank and moved away.

Where have I come? Franz wondered.

And there was nowhere to go to escape from such cold. The Russian peasants lived in small, stone huts with thatched roofs and wooden-shutter windows that the wind whistled through. Usually there was only one room with a single fireplace, and the family would huddle close to it if there was anything to burn to make a fire.

Franz was traveling as guard on a supply train that derailed. The soldiers were parceled out to be housed with the villagers. Franz was to stay with a family that had three children.

He stepped into the doorway and looked at them. They all had blue eyes, like himself, but very pale and washed out. They squatted next to a fireplace full of dark, gray ashes that had not seen flame in days. He put down his shaving kit and pack, and spoke one of his few Russian phrases, "A fire?" Hoping to warm his hands.

"Since your coming, there is nothing to burn," the father answered in guttural German. "There was never much to burn, but it was enough to get us through the winters. Now there is nothing, to burn or to eat or to wear."

He then lapsed into silence. The children and woman stared at Franz. Behind them, in the darkest half of the cottage, a rough, cracked rock wall stood more or less upright as the far edge to the family's space. Once, the other side of it had probably held their cow or goats or chickens, whatever little bit this family had had.

Now it was empty and dark and stank of being the family latrine.

Franz stood there, looking at what Gunter had described the day he came back to the college, and told of the poverty and want in Poland that he had been helping to wipe out.

Now Franz stood in front of this family and thought that it was two years later and there was no change. *But it was coming. It had to be coming.* Germany had said it was bringing it.

They gave him the spot beneath the window for sleeping. The snow would blow in and settle onto his neck and ear. He stayed in that hut for eleven days, and then a train had arrived for him.

In that time, the family did not eat or move, except for infrequent trips to the latrine. They sat and stared at Franz whenever he was inside, as though he were something they could not recognize. Even more, as though he was something they had no wish to know, as though they looked on animal entrails, or the meatless carcass left from a feast.

When he came back from patrol on his final night there, the father was sitting in Franz' sleeping place in the last light of the window. At Franz' entry, he jumped up and moved hurriedly to the fireplace, dropping in his haste what he had been doing. Franz looked down at it and discovered a worn, thin bladed knife and two tiny horses carved from some kind of bone. The detail was beautiful.

Franz offered him the last silver mark he had. He raised his chin. He was willing to sell, yes, but what else would he give? Franz looked at him, and of its own, his hand crept to his neck and pulled the chain that held his cross.

He looked horrified and then nodded. Even God could be traded for if it would feed his children. *No, that he would not take.* But when Franz added his watch, he looked pleased and the trade was sealed. The small horses had fine features, eyeballs carved within the lids and a tiny feathering on their fetlocks, reminding Franz of the draft horses at home. Barter among the troops was common. Items such as these had bought him a small stash of cigarettes or chocolate on the rare times they were available. He had not thought of life before as being traded, but that is what he gave this father. Food, if he could find it, for a few more days of living.

Later, much later, at Camp Penn, Franz' hut was hung with wooden shutters against the ocean wind that could come up so quickly. Then he thought back to the shutters of that earlier hovel, and he dreamed of the staring blue eyes. The look of completely giving up.

He would lie in his bunk and come awake, having dreamt of the empty, cold fireplace and the pale gaze of the family watching him. He would waken, thinking he was cold or hungry, but, upon self-examination, would be neither.

But that would be much later.

Just after the handshake of their trade that night, shouting erupted in the street outside. A much-needed supply train had arrived, and Franz went to help unload the tents and foodstuffs and ammunition that were needed so badly. He walked along the snow path of the village, and on reaching the train saw a knot of men standing idle by the track.

"What is happening?" he greeted them. "We should be getting to work so that we have a warm meal and sleeping place for tonight." He looked up at the gray sky, trying to measure the amount of daylight left. "We want to be finished before dark."

"We are standing because there is nothing to unload," a sergeant said in answer to his question. Franz pointed at one man handing a box from the open door of a train car to a man on the ground.

"Some are working," he said.

"Yes, but there is not much more than that to unload," the sergeant answered a second time. He shrugged his shoulders and looked at Franz. "I do not know what it matters to you, anyway, Becker."

"Why do you say that?" Franz was stung.

"Because your name is on the transport list to go back. By evening you will be chugging toward home. We will still be here."

And in a sudden rush that was what happened. He gathered his shaving kit, and jacket and rifle and was bundled into a troop car by dark. They began to work their way to the southwest, back toward Germany and home! Excitement grew in the cars as they moved along. Many of these troops had not been home in over two years.

The troop car was full, and the men slept as best they could. It was two days before the chill began to break. With each click of the wheels, Franz began to feel more German again.

After the cold silence of the people and the way of living so wild, so simply focused on existing, it had begun to seem as though the country, the home he remembered, was a fairy place, like the fabled stories and people of the Black Forest.

Home. On the eighth day of the train trip, a ripple ran through the car. The next stop would be Elenruhe, Franz's own small town. A wave of excitement raced through him. Eve and Pieter were here in their small flat. He gathered his things and jumped from the car as it stopped. He was given a four-hour pass to say hello to his family and then ordered to be back at the camp.

Before he left camp, he took his first shower in months and carefully shaved and dressed. He received a newer uniform and asked if he could have one that had not been worn before.

"No, we are keeping those for the winter troops," he was told. "You will not need such heavy things where you are going." It was an odd comment, but he did not follow up on it, so intent was his desire to see Eve and Pieter.

Once dismissed, he raced through the small town, not thinking of how he must look. He threw open the street door and raced up the stairs, boots echoing on each one. He knocked on the upper door, the front door to their flat, and called, "It is me, I am home!" Eve opened the door quickly and stood looking at him, amazed. She had been cooking and the smell of sautéed onions made him hungry.

She rushed at once into his arms with a funny squeak, as though her words were stuck, at last asking, "How is it that you are here?"

He explained about the four hours and that he must leave again. She moved to the side. Behind her, crouching just under the edge of a dining table that was really too big for the room, was a little boy. Pieter. His son. Franz bent down, and his pistol dug into his leg. Quickly, he removed it and knelt again, so as not to appear so big.

"Pieter," he said. "I am your father." The child looked back at him and then up at Eve. In his hands he clutched two wooden spoons, cooking like his mother.

His eyes were big and blue and beautiful. Franz thought briefly how different they were from the pale, washed out eyes of the children he had just left. Then he shoved that thought from his mind. He had less than four hours and wanted to come to know his son as much as he could.

Eve watched for a moment, then took down a picture of Franz from the table. She knelt and said to Pieter, "Liebchen, who is this?" She pointed at the picture, and the boy's gaze followed her finger. He thought for a moment.

A sunny smile lit his face and he came to lean against his mother's knee, putting a chubby finger on the face beneath the glass. Franz's face. "Papa," he said clearly. "That is my Papa."

"And this is Papa," Eve said tenderly. "He has come to visit you, just like we ask for every night at our prayers."

She pushed him gently in front of her, toward Franz. He wanted to take Pieter in his arms and hold him, but knew that if he moved first, his son would be frightened, and then all of the time would be lost, the little bit of it that they had. Instead, Franz turned to dig in his shaving kit and found the two small horses he had traded for on his last night on the eastern front. He held them out to his son.

Pieter looked at them, entranced, and his small hands reached out and took the tiny figures from Franz' palm. "Oh," he said to Eve. "H'oss." And he smiled wide with delight.

The blue eyes moved to Franz, and for a moment the smile switched off. Then the smile came back and he crossed to Franz.

"Papa," Pieter said, and put a finger in his mouth. "Papa come," he said to his mother. At this tiny voice saying "Papa," a sweet high tingle coursed through Franz.

"Yes, Papa came," he said, and Franz's throat grew tight. A picture may be an image, but it does not hold the breathing, the warmth, the reality of seeing someone alive.

No moment would ever be as deep for him as that first time his son called him Papa.

He was very glad he had traded away his silver and his watch for something to give his son that would stay here longer than himself.

The moments went too quickly, and in no time he was standing on the small landing outside their door, promising to write and to come back safely. He wanted badly to stay, but he was a soldier first, then, and a good one. He was needed by his country.

Chapter 21

Franz arrived at the station to find a train rumbling and chuffing, almost ready to pull out. It was facing south. Curious. He had thought he would be going back to the front or maybe into France.

But he was sent to Africa, to assist the Afrikakorps - the special, select and earnest ones. These soldiers had often been zealous members of the Youth Group when they were small boys. The Youth Group had been like a warm and supportive family. The hard lessons were introduced a bit at a time, so that they never really saw them for the big steps that they were. By the time the boys reached the other side, they were toughened without ever knowing how they had become so ruthless.

Africa was a different place. Very hot and cold by turn, it had this beat he could feel everywhere. Like a giant throbbing, primitive and strong, so that he felt it in his own body, like his heart. But deeper.

He felt it at night when he was alone, on patrol, or in his tent. Others felt it, and it seemed to excite them. To make them more crazy and more determined to kill.

And they did, kill and rape and burn and destroy. All in the Fuhrer's name. And the more they destroyed, the more they were praised. And the dark and different natives took the killing and punishing in silence. But in the night, white throats would be cut and things taken. The Germans never did find out by whom or how.

But for that year, the AfrikaKorps went on its way, cutting a swath through cities and people, so that all would know they were there. They did not lose a battle, nor a position. Confidence was their armor, without a chink and invincible.

They held strongest in Northwest Africa, wide and empty. Then they lost at Tobruk, and the tide of the war began to change.

Rommel came and said it was not the war that was changing, but that battles had been lost. Their unit was called back. Whole lines were retreating across the sands, leaving a tideline's jagged edge of equipment and boots and cans discarded from food behind them as they went. Sometimes they disabled the equipment or buried the cans, but the sand shifts in the desert, and their path was often uncovered two days after their passing.

The numbers of abandoned pieces amazed Franz. But, as the kommandant explained, much of it was beyond repair. The harshness of the sand and heat took a heavy toll. Parts stayed so hot after use. And they were used a lot. The Allies had become very tenacious, very driven at their fighting.

That was different from the start of the war. Then it took the Allies a long while to regroup after being beaten. They had seemed almost numbed by the destruction fighting caused. Then the Allies got wily and began to catch and hold the supply trains. It became hard to get items of all kinds - food, water, ammunition, and clothes. They diverted several trains that were to come, one right after the other. And twice they bombed and sank ships before they even reached the harbor. The Allies were becoming smarter, Franz thought, at figuring out what the Germans might do.

Patrols increased, and they worked hot days and cold nights with little food or rest.

Mail and communications had been pared down to the essentials. Franz would sit with his gun against his cheek, and it would either freeze or burn his skin, depending on whether it was day or night. He looked at the desert rolling away in dunes as far as he could see. For long, slow hours he did nothing but sit, staring ahead at the empty sands.

Some of the men grew hardened even more by this, became more determined. It was as though the more they lost of lives and land and things, the cockier and crueler they became. Franz thought of home, realizing that he had not heard in a very long time how they were or what they were doing.

Then they left Africa and moved back toward Europe, crossing back across the places they had come through with so much confidence and speed two years before. Now they traveled at night, using the dark to cloak their movements.

He saw plentiful water for the first time in a year when they did a night crossing back to the point of San Carlo on the most southern part of Italy. Franz thought it funny how quickly that part of the world went from desert to the trees and valleys of Europe.

They headed north and he kept waking, expecting to see distances, but he did not, for the hills got in the way. He kept feeling trapped, had grown more accustomed than he realized to the long distances of his last year.

His unit took up patrol in some low hills, in the short days of winter. He drew watch duty that first night in a new place, with a new man, Gus. It was dark and cold, and Franz kept slipping on rocks the rain had loosened. Each time he moved, he sent stones rattling down the hill. Just below, where the bluff had been notched out by water cutting through, was a hut. The roof was thatch and old pieces of rusted metal laid out across its slant to keep the rain out.

Every time the rocks tumbled down a few of them would slide down onto the roof, and clank and skip off of the wet grass and metal.

And a donkey would bray and move about. The poor beast must have circled a thousand times, round and round in his pen. Then he would stand and stare up at Franz, making a high-pitched squeal.

An old woman who lived in the cottage kept opening the door, and he could see straight into the room. There was no hall or back porch, just the one room. Not much, just a square of yellow light and a straight chair set next to the fire.

The fire was burning bright, and the smoke smelled both of the pine being burned and something she was stewing over the flames.

They sat and watched her, the rain running into their collars, hair and eyes. Their cloaks leaked through, and they shivered inside the soaked layers. Gus leaned toward him, and even though they were under orders not to talk, he breathed in Franz' ear, "What do you think she is cooking?"

Franz lifted his nose and sniffed hungrily. Definitely meat of some kind; the smell was rich and heavy, like the smell of good gravy in a boat to be served with a silver ladle and butter and soft rolls.

Chicken, he decided and told Gus so. "Chicken with tiny dumplings floating in the gravy."

"I thought lamb," Gus whispered back.

Then a cold piece of steel touched Franz ear, and a voice said, "Hands up."

English words, ones he would learn by heart.

The Americans had found them, and they were taken prisoner. He re-climbed the hill at gunpoint. In a clearing, the headlights of a jeep shone on most of their battalion. They were shoved together inside a circle of American soldiers who were talking quietly.

One of the German troops answered every question very loudly, and then said to the American, "You are being watched. You will die at the next moment."

The American captain lowered his gun and waited for the bullets to take him, but the only sound was the rain in the trees. He looked back at his enemy, straight in the eyes.

When the war started, the Americans made many mistakes, some from not having fought before, and many just from fear. That was early in the war, but now this captain showed how much had changed. It did not bother him to see someone shot, and if he died, others from his side would take the enemy out. He had quit believing in Germany's power, and had begun to believe in his own.

They marched into the rain for the rest of the night.

"That old woman was cooking grass," Franz's captain reported the Americans said. "Grass."

"Do not believe that," the German captain said loudly. But Franz learned later that it was so. Even after many years, he remembered that. He did not know from where came that rich smell of meat.

They were taken back through Italy on a train, to where the United States had gotten a toe-hold on the land along the islets of southern France.

The train was dark and crowded, and he dreaded where they were going. He rode all night trying to guess how far from home he was at each moment. They were very cold.

The American compound was big, a sea of pens. There were long rows of chain link and wire netting runs with roofs on them with strands of heavy, barbed wire along the tops of the fences. These had been hastily put up to handle all of the soldiers who had been captured. German soldiers.

The men running the compound were like the wire. They were thin and didn't look as though they had had rest or food in any extra measure for a long time. They moved constantly. The prisoners were processed in and their papers taken away.

On the way to the shower, Franz heard that 17,000 soldiers were captured that night. Around him was doubt, believe it or not, though here they were as prisoners.

He had his first bath in a month, and then food that was not one of the meals given for field use. It was rice and gravy, thick and warm. And he could have a second bowl. He wolfed the first one, gravy running down his chin, and slowed for the second helping.

As he was eating it, someone said, "Have you heard? We are being moved out."

"Where to?" Franz asked.

"To America," he answered. "We are going to America."

Franz dropped his bowl then and ran to the fence, and stood looking at the hills. He kept thinking he could see a tiny glimmer of lights in the low places where the train track threaded from the wide fields where he was kept, to Elenruhe. For the camp was not far from his village. He was almost all the way home. Just not the way he had planned to be.

He put out his hand and grasped the barbed wire, not gently. Hard. There was pain and pressure and then with a pop, the point of wire entered his skin and the metal smell of blood rose to his nose, sharp and sudden.

"Here now," a voice said behind him, causing him to jump. No one else was here behind the tents. "You don't want to be hurting your hand now."

Franz listened to the accent, odd and rolling, not understanding any of the words. His visitor was redheaded and stocky, with a face that looked open and fresh.

"Back now." The soldier motioned Franz back to the tents with the point of his rifle.

There, a man was speaking inside a circle of listeners. "No one wishes to speak German here. We are prisoners, despised. I hear that it will go hard for us, they will probably be wanting to starve us to death. I hear that they got to some camps in Germany and opened them up to find stacks of bodies and living skeletons."

"Where was this?" Franz asked.

"In Poland, and the East, mostly," the speaker answered, and then moved restlessly away.

The next morning, suddenly, an American private came through the tent before sunrise. He ordered them up and to wash and eat and gather their things. Papers were required to be out and at the ready. This was a trick. The papers had not been returned.

The prisoners were placed into long columns and marched to the docks. Around him were men in lines so far you could see no end. Guards with machine guns sat on trucks above the crowds. A man walked back and forth in between them and yelled in bad German.

"Stay in your place in line. If anyone tries to run, the machine gunners will open fire in that area of the crowd. And you will die. Not just the runner, but all of those around him, too. And silence. Talking is forbidden."

Next to Franz, a man spoke, as though he would not follow any American's order. "They are so desperate it is pitiful. They are trying to goad us into moving so they can shoot us on the spot."

"Why are they desperate?" Franz asked. He wanted to believe the man, but the Americans did not act scared or rushed or desperate. To him they seemed confident and sure.

"Because we are going to America," the man answered scornfully. "And they do not want to have to take us there, because their country is barely hanging on. They do not want us to see that, because they are afraid of our spies. And when our spies report back how their efforts are thin and rickety, then the Americans know we will see their recent victories as flukes and that we will win this war!" He finished speaking in a shout. An American soldier worked his way toward them.

The line inched forward, and Franz looked for a chance to escape. If he could make the shipside, could he jump and swim between other ships and get aground with no one seeing? No chance came. The hold of the ship opened and they were pressed in. Franz watched the blue sky as long as he could. Watched the edges of it around the door grow smaller and smaller as the door closed. And with a clang it went dark.

He felt like he would jump out of his skin. He wanted to run to the door, to beat and claw it open.

They moved down through the deck levels and then up again. At last they reached a narrow corridor and were put into cabins. He looked around. The walls were done in paneled wood and the railings were polished brass. This ship had once been a cruise vessel made for pleasure voyages.

The cabin that he was to share with five others was small. There was a strong metal grill over the porthole, with a heavy canvas covering in front of it on the outside. This was a precaution, so that they could not signal out the window at night and perhaps attract attention.

They were marched to supper in the ballroom. Dinner was cheese sandwiches. But you could have several and the bread did not have mold or worms. Then they were locked in for the night. Franz lay there and listened to the others breathing in the dark. He could hardly breathe, much less sleep.

He had not seen anyone shot or beaten, had not heard screams of pain or fright when interrogation occurred. And it was occurring. The men were taken one at a time and spoken to in a small room. That went on the whole trip, but he never heard that what they learned was of value.

And so they crossed. Their days were marked by meals and two daily exercise times, when some of them were let out on the deck. American GIs with guns stood every few feet along the rail and watched closely. Their orders were to shoot for the slightest cause.

He was walking the deck when a ripple of voices ran through the ship. Land ho. Franz felt a coldness sweep through him. This was real, after all. He was about to be on their land.

He swallowed hard just as a great cheering went up from the front of the ship.

He heard the American wounded soldiers on board had caught sight of their Statue of Liberty. Around him, many soldiers spit and boasted how they would come back and blow her head off when the Fatherland came for them. *For even now,* they said, *German submarines and warships were chasing in our wake, lurking just far enough behind that the radar could not find them. It would only be a matter of days until the Germans came to free them and to bomb America out of existence.*

Suddenly a soldier appeared with a rifle and motioned Franz's group toward the stairs.

His breath shortened as he ducked and went down the narrow stairs. As he passed the dining room, the mirrors along the other wall caught and threw back a reflection of his line of men. Many of them wore parts of their original uniforms mixed in with an assortment of coveralls and workpants. Almost all of them wore plain, black shoes. Behind them, the carved mahogany mantle rose to the ceiling, where the giant chandelier burned overhead. Such a ship was made for dancing, and stars, and the ocean. For good music and good wine. The ragtag men did not belong. His stomach twisted so hard a flash of heat ran through him.

Fear is not the German way. His kommandant's voice echoed so loudly in his ear that he started and turned to look hurriedly, almost expecting to see those bright, burning eyes somewhere just behind his shoulder. *Master it, that is how you will win, will not be captured. That is not the German way, either. The best are not imprisoned.*

They were locked into their cabin. A grinning soldier took the cover off their cabin porthole, knocking and pointing at the harbor, showing them his home.

The horn sounded through the ship with a vibration. Three more short blasts, answered by another horn. All six of them crammed the porthole at once, at last giving into a line so one could look at a time.

"Do you see many ships?"

The horn sounded again on a lower note, and then a third time. Through a tiny gap in the canvas, they could see the forward motion of the ship lessen, and a tug move in to help lead the ship toward a narrow place along one of the docks.

The blue water was choppy, with bits of white topping the waves. Franz closed his eyes and imagined how the wind felt.

"There is that statue," Heinrich, a heavyset machinist said, "I heard we shot its arm off."

"The Statue of Liberty," someone said from the back of the press to the window. "That is the right name."

Franz leaned close to the window, as close as he could and looked up, sideways at the statue. It slid into view, then the sun and water disappeared behind her gowned figure. They were passing almost directly beneath.

"It still has the arm, and a lamp and feet," he said. "There does not look to be anything missing. I do not think we blew anything off of it."

The lock clicked behind them, and Franz heard the scrape of the hasp being taken off, and then the door swung open. Two American GIs with guns stood there.

"Gather your belongings," one of them ordered in halting German. "Be quick about it."

They filed off the ship in a large, crowded huddle, like an insect with many feet that kept tripping over each other. Just beyond the dock, a line of stake bed trucks waited and they were loaded onto those.

Beyond the trucks, the city began, people and houses and small stores scattered just hundreds of feet away. He watched in amazement at the people who were moving freely along the street, in and out of doorways, crossing a street at the whistle and wave of a large uniformed man on a horse.

The German government had told the troops how hard the war had been on America. That the cities were full of bombed and empty-eyed buildings where people lived in the remains of basements or garages and dug in the trash for food.

Franz got a place along the edge of the back of the truck. When they began to move, he held on tight, watching closely. He wanted to see as much of the enemy as he could.

They rode for a few hours, and then the line of trucks pulled into what looked to be a great train yard. There were many trucks like the one they had come in, and many small buildings, also.

They were taken off the trucks, and lined up and sorted according to lists that the Americans held in their hands. Franz got in line with three of his cabin mates, Karl and Johann and Dmitri, determined that they would stay together. But he was shunted into one line and they, another. In his own bunch, he saw the short loud man named Willi Prang, who had been the "cage boss" in France, the go-between for captives and captors.

It crept on toward evening mealtime, and the American soldiers passed through, tossing things into the groups of men sitting on the ground.

He heard then a familiar voice, and recognized the redheaded soldier who had spoken to him in France.

"See ya." The redheaded sergeant grinned as he tossed two small cans of food at Franz's feet.

Franz dove for them and got one in each fist as he rose, looking after the retreating back.

Later that night, he spoke to Willi Prang, who seemed to have talked a bit with the Americans. "Willi, you speak a little English."

"Ja, but not much. I have never wanted to know such a useless thing." Willi lit a cigarette and drew the smoke deep into his lungs. "Why?" Willi spoke between puffs.

"I want to know what one of the guards is saying to me."

"What is that?"

"What does it mean, this 'see ya'? Is he trying to say something in our language? Something with 'ja'?"

Willi snorted, "No, you idiot, he is saying he will be back later, saying goodbye, but in a casual way."

"Why does he bother with that?" he asked.

The cage boss did not give an answer.

Chapter 22

One of the first things Franz learned in America was that it was the donkey that gave them away. One of the Americans had grown up in a Northern state on a dairy farm. There they ran donkeys in with the cattle, to give notice of bears or moose in the woods where the cattle foraged.

That man recognized the sound the donkey made when they sensed an enemy. But this enemy wasn't bears or moose; it was the smell of the African pack donkeys and camels that had become ground into the Germans' clothes and gear. The rain and dampness that night released the smells and drifted them down to the donkey. And so he told his owner.

Franz thought a thousand times of that night, that maybe African and Italian donkeys did not like each other any more than the African and Italian people he met. Thought of the slim chance of someone knowing the call of a donkey that signals something was wrong.

Camp Penn, Cape Cod, 1944

There were many camps, all built much the same. The German prisoners were shuttled between them, separated and moved out often, sometimes as soon as a truck appeared, empty and ready to be loaded. They followed the need for work, harvest, logging, and building. It became a blur. At the last camp, they seemed to settle quickly.

It really would not be very hard to escape, he decided, after walking the camp twice round. The corner towers and double strand barbed wire were tough, fearsome by American standards. But to a Nazi German, they were what Americans called "a piece of cake."

When he looked around, he could see holes in every part of the prison walls. Valiant but inadequate efforts at protecting themselves from...him. And yet, the local people who worked at the camp had been nothing but kindness.

The very absurdity of that was what finally penetrated the coldness - the dark, icy part of him. The part that had watched his own people torture and kill for a reason. Reasons he had once willingly accepted.

This camp was for Nazis only, for the truest believers in a now-tottering and shambling cause. Other Germans were other places. Because of that, he had come here thinking that this would be the toughest and the grimmest of the American prison camps. Cold and hunger like he had known once, captured and waiting in a field near Alencon, France.

Instead, these simple, good people tried so hard to be decent with blankets and food. They did not know how to be vile. When they built the camp they did not know how awful awfulness can be. The gritty foul-tasting kind of bile that comes from being raised with it. To have it bred and read into you along with your evening milk and swimming in the Blausee.

Here he began to recall walking in the green soft German spring that made the awfulness of the war a never-could-happen thing.

He woke in the night, in the silent hours when the seconds only move at half-speed and carry with them long moments of memory that fade in the brightest sun.

He pulled the rough wool blanket closer under his chin against the chill that always crept in. But he didn't get any warmer, because the chill didn't come from outside. He kept thinking of the eyes of an old man who had given away their position in a stone-walled village, of the utter, mindless terror that they could not hush or stop. In that last moment of being the predator, for the only moment in all his time in the war, he had seen what it cost those they were conquering.

There had been terror, deep and complete in the old man's eyes, but beneath that there had also been hatred, as though he were looking on the devil.

Franz closed his eyes and breathed slow and deep. One of the soldiers who came from the camps he was hearing of now spoke of captives holding their breath in tight places, to make the living go on a bit longer.

Supposedly, in these camps, thousands were being put to death. For what did they hold their breath, then? To be killed in the gas instead? The man speaking of it had laughed harshly. Others laughed with him, and Franz turned as if to get more coffee and passed on through the door. Outside, he threw the steaming brew across the gray night. It fell in a hissing arc on the fresh snow, melting into the drift, cutting away the clean white surface.

He kept dreaming of the crucifix he had given to the Russian father, coming alive to stare at him when he knelt for the camp pastor's absolution. It was always at 2:00 a.m., when the tiny eyes of the cross burned bright and clear, full of a knowing that brought him awake.

Each morning he looked in the mirrors above the sink while washing in a row of men. He looked the same in the sunrise as he had always looked in the mirror, but he did not know how that could be so.

The long rank of naked, jostling men pushed any further thinking from his mind. He hurried to dress and breakfast, always trying to eat to fill the gnawing in his stomach that grew worse in the night.

Other things stayed on the edge of his mind, peeping out when he did not expect them. Part of him went on with living his days. He worked in the camp kitchen, making great pots of soup to ladle out to each prisoner along with hunks of white bread.

The bread was soft and moist, brought each day in a variety of baskets and wooden carry boxes by a group of women. They wore old, patched clothes and men's jackets against the dark cold of the mornings, hair pulled back and tied, heavy boots on their feet.

They worked, were not soft-handed and well-dressed, like the women of home, but they never failed to make him think of Eve. Remembering, he would stand at the long wooden counter, chopping mountains of potatoes, onions and whatever other vegetables had been delivered.

At that time of the morning, the soup vats were already smoking with the meat and soup stock started over the fires. Coffee stood ready in big pots for the guards and delivery people and the prisoners who had early camp detail.

And a great mound of rolls were grabbed and wolfed down with the coffee by the morning jostle of people, hands and cups of detainer and detainee slaking their common hunger in those dark early hours.

One morning, for the first time, he spoke to one of the women who always brought the bread.

"Good morning," he said slowly, working on the English words.

She glanced at him, surprised, bobbing her head in return. Contact between camp staff and prisoners was not encouraged, but what was the harm in a few words?

"Morning," she said, continuing to take the bread out of the basket at her elbow and laying each loaf, golden and long, on a clean, white cloth stretched along the middle of a serving table.

"You are baking all of this each day?" His words were slow.

She smiled. "No. Some of the village women bake it at home, then I pick it up and bring it to the camp. Spreading out the baking is the only way there is enough for all of you."

She looked up and saw that her words were lost. He could not follow the English that fast. "We want you to not be hungry," she said.

"Yes," Franz said. That he could understand. She left then, and he went on chopping vegetables and simmering them in the kettle. After cooking, he began to clean up, washing each knife and spoon and pot in hot, steamy water until all were shiny and ready for the next day's work.

From midmorning on, he helped to build things in a cluttered yard of sorts. Here he and other men scrounged and pieced together to make things for the camp. Metal was at a premium and they used what they could find. Behind their work area was a dumpground of unused equipment, old barrels and pieces of wood. The barrel rims could be torn off, washed, and used to frame many items. His job was to wash the pieces of metal and get them clean. It was a hard job - the metal flaked away in big pieces, and sometimes he scrubbed a long time before finding a solid surface beneath.

He went to bed tired, but not to sleep. A part of him stayed awake and restless, always. It was as though one of him, as an observer, watched the planning and actions of the other. He lived more in his dreams then, than in the confines of his real world, hemmed in as he was by, first, wire, then the pressing close pines and, always, by memories.

He dreamt of the old logging road. In his sleep it took on a ghostly, whitish glow, a luminescence that shown brighter than the crushed shell base did in the daytime.

He dreamed of setting foot on it and following it to the end. Somewhere in its turnings, it left a lumber camp in New England and wound over the hills of Germany and down into his village beyond.

He would wake then in a sweat and reach for his wallet, to open it and touch the picture of Eve and Pieter.

In his dream, Eve stayed just beyond sight. He could hear the sound of her voice but not the words. It went on and on and he would listen, trying to hear what she spoke of, thinking then he would know what time of day it was.

But he would waken and remember the wallet had been taken along with his book of who he was and where he was from. The *soldbuch*, the proof of himself and being German.

His stomach grippe worsened. He became a regular sight to the night guards. Each evening, at about 11:00 he ran for the latrine. At first they stopped and questioned him, but soon learned they did not want to know what he did in the small, cold building on his midnight rushes for relief. He continued to be ill, strange bouts of bleeding coming now with his straining.

They smoked and spoke softly in the guard towers and outside the wire the forest lay dark and silent.

Occasionally a truck would rattle by on the road, shifting gears as it left the camp, but the sound soon faded into the trees.

The trip to the latrine was a must, but once there, with things taken care of, the trip back was slower. As he walked back to the tent, he could feel the gauntlet of eyes from the night watchers. Taunts would float quietly on the air: "Miss your 'kraut, huh, boy?" He could not follow the words, but the tones were not kind. He liked better the kindness of the woman in the kitchen.

He began to plan, putting together two things that made more of a difference together than apart. He started by watching a bit each night as he made his way back from the latrine.

New prisoners were brought in evenings, as much as in the daytime. The lights of the camp burned all night. They were mounted on tall posts, rigged high above the platforms upon which the guards stood. The globes burned with a golden glow that grew fuzzy in the damp nights, so that it seemed as if each post held a giant woolen ball.

He watched and thought. The guards were looking out of the light, which would make the dark beyond even harder to see into. When the trucks arrived, usually just at dusk, there was a melee of shouting and movement as men were moved out and others moved in.

Trustees with lists loaded groups of men and counted heads before announcing to the Americans that the trucks' cargo was accounted for. The mess tent served big meals to the men coming and going. Those being moved out left with a full stomach for the trip; those coming ate while they were being checked in.

The papers for the men continued to be taken up. They were kept in a back office, held in separate bundles to go with groups of men. But they were not bound together and occasionally he saw one slide away from its pile. *Would there ever be a chance that one could disappear*, he wondered.

The second part came unexpectedly one night, when the count was off, lists so scribbled and torn that half the back page and the totals were missing.

He only overheard it by chance, but sometimes the happening of a second changes the course of a lifetime. Before he even quite knew it, he had on the jacket and cap of a new arrival, and he stepped in line to get on the last truck in the line.

The first loaded and soonest out, he had decided, left the least chance for being noticed.

After it pulled out, Franz swung down and moved along beside the wheels. Now a bit of recognition was handy; he was often seen about. But not at this job.

He ran next to the truck as it trundled out the gate, but on the opposite side, as though he would help to swing the gate shut. Gear shifted, canvas flapped and he grabbed the truck body so close in the shadow of the tire that rubber brushed his cheek.

He hung on for the count of ten, forty yards, he estimated, until the tree-line began. At ten, he let go and shoved backwards, somersaulting into the grass and flattening himself, expecting to be found.

But the tail-lights grew smaller, and the camp settled back into its routine, the guards going in for their supper in shifts. He could not believe his luck; he rose to his knees and moved into the woods. He stopped then in the first screen of pines and looked back, thinking that stillness was harder to see than movement, even in the shadows.

The lights of the camp burned on, and the quiet voices of the guards drifted in the still air. He held his breath and slid quietly to the next tree, stepping into the narrow shadow of its trunk.

Silence answered him back. He listened but the stillness around him held no other living thing. The pines had no animals rustling in them tonight.

One hundred yards beyond the light, he broke into a run. He could wait no more, could not be caught now, could not stay inside that wire another day. He ran from tree to tree, his gait shuffling and uneven. The strength he had gathered on the good food had disappeared. He grabbed at the sudden pain in his side and went on. He had not run full out in all the time of his captivity. It would take time before his body would remember how to use the muscles long untaxed.

The ache in his side grew hot and sharp, like a knife beneath his ribs.

Just a cramp. He leaned against a small pine for a moment to ease the pain.

Only his hoarse gulps for air sounded in the snowy silence that folded around him. He swallowed hard and tried to still his breathing enough to hear if anyone pursued him.

Snow was a funny medium, he had learned well in childhood. The nearest things were muffled, but sounds farthest away echoed and carried among the swirling flakes, so that people you would not have guessed heard things you would not have imagined, nor wanted them to know.

Now his fear was that as he drew farther from the camp, the crunching snow would give him away, bring searchers right to him.

His eyes darted at a sound that made him freeze. A dog's bay, distorted and bouncing from one rock wall to the other echoed along behind him. He shoved himself away from the tree trunk.

His breathing grew harsher, and sweat began to run down his temples. Blood ran from his nose, a trickle, and then a stream.

He fell, faint, and his last thoughts were of walking up a stone walk to a timbered cottage bright with spring flowers. May in Germany, soft and sweet. He could almost taste the air. Hotness rose in his throat, and the sweetness vanished like sugar scorched.

His last thought as he fell was that the dog was in front of him, not after, not chasing. He had escaped them, was safe, and was going home.

Slowly, the cold, clean air slowed the bleeding from his nose and mouth. He slept in a dark huddle on the frozen ground until dawn, when the thin high call of birds reached through the haze and woke him. He rose and stumbled toward the rising sun.

He did not get very far.

****

Emmet Nelson always rose at daybreak; the sputter of his old truck coming in fits and starts as the ancient vehicle trundled slowly along the sandy track toward Rachel's Corner.

As he eased through the turn in the road, a figure on the ground caught his eye. Emmet Nelson leaned out the window and looked closer. Behind him, the bay glimmered through the trees. As the wind turned, a warning buoy clanged on the tide. Another fine Cape day was dawning, the early fog chased out to sea as the breeze freshened into the sunrise.

He stopped the truck and climbed stiffly down. The figure had not moved, and he limped stiffly up beside it and nudged gently with his toe. Still no response.

"Damn sailors," he grunted and knelt down. The base behind him and the bay beyond were responsible for more people in these woods than he had seen in many a year. He sighed and rolled the man over, squatted and studied the young face.

The chin was covered with dirty blond stubble split by a livid purple welt and dried blood that had dribbled from the chin to cover the front of a threadbare, woven shirt that had once been brown.

A lot of blood, no question. He reached for a pulse and found one, rapid and uneven. Drink was often the problem; the men did not wake and the ship sailed. It had happened a lot of times, and the men stayed and worked until they could catch their own again, or take passage on another for home.

Pushing and pulling, he rolled the limp body onto the low trailer he pulled behind his truck. Like most folks in the isolated houses along the bay, Emmet went to town once a week for his supplies. Today he had gotten corn and hay for the few cattle he kept, so the trailer was pretty full. But there was room - there was always room if someone needed something.

Those were the teachings of the steepled white frame church just down from Emmet's house. *It had been easier, before the world began to grow in on itself, to be true to the church teachings,* he had thought for some time.

These days you never knew who would be found along the beaches or roads of this once quiet, isolated place. Emmet had long used that quiet as a backdrop for the watercolors he painted of a war he still tried to leave behind, on the other side of the ocean, on the other end of life.

But still it got up with him in the mornings, when the fledgling Air Force base down the road and through the trees began the flight testing of planes for this latest war, one that he was now too old to fight. He had never quit looking for the planes to fly out of the sunrise, like those that had taken his unit, all but himself.

Still, he was a damn sight healthier than others. He had all his legs and arms, and he could make the daybreak cheery. It just took a little work.

He wrestled the young man from the trailer and dragged him, none too gently, into his small house to a low bed in a backroom off the kitchen.

Emmet had learned long ago, in WWI, that the body can take a good bit. For awhile. Heaving the limp body onto the bed, Emmet stood up, his breathing hoarse, rasping for air.

What language to try? Foreign sailors happened several times a year here. Norwegian failed, but Danish produced a quiver, then a lapse again into unconsciousness, heavy and deep.

Emmet considered, and then went about his work. Small farms had only a few men who worked them now; most younger ones were off to the fighting.

At noon the stranger still slept, and at three and at six, when the sun fell and Emmet came inside to a supper of chowder and coffee.

After supper he drowsed in his chair, catching up a bit for the midnight check he would have to do on the ponds, to make sure the water levels were still right. The cranberries would freeze without the flooding. As he worked his feet into old, cracked boots a slight movement on the bed caught his eye.

He moved over to see him better and found a pair of eyes watching.

"Evening," he said. The eyes watched on.

Emmet tried again. "Are you better?"

Still watching.

"English?" This time a slight shake of the head.

He tried the Danish of that morning and the eyes lit up a little.

So his visitor was "from away."

They settled into a routine, two men bound by their own rememberings, into a life that suited both of them. Emmet spoke little but English and the stranger always answered "ja," so that Emmet would say, "I know, you're going to ja'n me. Just go on and do it."

And the stranger would comply, doing the work quietly and carefully. Emmet started to call him Jan, said Yahn, ready for the yes answer he always got. They became a habit to each other, company in the quiet nights by the fire and in the chilly rounds of the bogs and barns with only the moon to see. It never really came up for Jan to leave. The time never seemed to arrive.

For a last name he took Neuman. Jan Neuman. Emmet didn't seem to notice, for Jan that was good enough.

Emmet began to tire as 1945 became 1946. The long days became longer as he slowed. An extra pair of hands wouldn't be amiss now that the cranberries were coming ripe. And there were the cows to care for; he wouldn't mind someone else forking hay for a while. He seemed to have a heaviness to him that he couldn't shake.

He needed the help, and it didn't seem right to turn a young man out who had worked hard and well for nothing but his board in those early years.

The young man got better, though well wouldn't ever describe him. He would start bleeding suddenly and go on until Emmet thought that surely there could be no more blood in him. Then he would get better and go on about his chores.

Eventually he took over all of Emmet's small farm chores. The life of a bogman was quiet, chill and lonely. It seemed to suit Jan.

So a Danish sailor he remained in Emmet's mind, at least. This didn't come about through lies, but through things he never said, truths he never spoke.

This silence, this double life was hard. He still waited, hoping for a chance to slip home. The first step would be to reach a city with ships that plied the ocean.

Jan's English bettered through Sundays spent scrubbing and polishing in the church kitchen. And he learned that there was a Red Cross office in Boston that had information gathered about the war and the people and countries, no matter who they were.

He decided on Boston.

He worked as hard and steadily as he could, so well that Emmet ceased to set his day's work, let him choose a schedule as he grew to know the feel of the bogs, each one a different face. In the fallow time of spring, Jan at last asked for a whole day off.

"Yes," Emmet said, "you can go now. Things are quiet, mostly." There was kindness in Emmet, but not extra. Jan could go because the bogs were silent and Emmet didn't need him, not because he had earned it.

"I thought to go to Boston," Jan said.

"Ayeh, to see someone in particular?" Emmet asked, eyes on the seining net he was mending that night.

"Not a person. I want to see what is there," Jan answered. *And what is there about home*, that piece he did not say. How could he say, I want to find out about a place no one mentions anymore? Germany had become a dirty word, spoken of only as something the Americans had conquered.

Emmet saw the practical side, "Your speaking will get better if you have to use it. That will be helpful in our busy times."

Even then he could see that the Cape was going to grow busier. There was money to be spent, and people were home from the war to spend it; more children than he had ever seen peopled the beaches and roadsides between the towns.

Jan made plans.

He worked it out carefully, taking the bus from two towns up so that there was not much chance of having to talk with anyone he might know.

Only one road ran through the Cape, but if he got onto the bus and settled into pretended sleep, maybe no one would recognize his face.

Jan dressed carefully in the blue jeans and flannel shirt that Capemen wore, and the short leather boots with cobbled soles. He dangled a cap with earflaps from one hand.

He waited in the early light, the only one to get on the bus. As he paid his fare, he worried that someone would see him counting his money, still slow at figuring which coins to use. But no one looked up from their reading, and he took a window seat halfway down the empty left side.

The doors hissed shut and the bus trundled and groaned toward Boston, full of people going to fill needs and enjoy a day in the city.

Chapter 23

The Red Cross office in Boston was in a restored firehouse, red brick with fresh white trim. Jan stood on the sidewalk in front of it, cap in hand. *No one knows me here,* he thought. And yet, fear squeezed his stomach tight.

Americans were not suspicious of questions, not the way they were at home, immediately thinking that you are asking for a reason that needs to be probed and reported. In his other life, he had been part of that. Part of the thing that now kept him up at night.

"Hello, may I help you?" A slender woman of twenty, with dark, bobbed hair unlocked the door with a jangle of keys against the knob.

"Yes, I need to check on some people." He shifted his cap to his other hand and held the door for her. The woman moved in past him and set her things on a desk.

"What country?" she asked.

"Germany," he said.

"Ah," she stepped back, and her eyes were distant now. "We don't have many records, so much was destroyed. And that country has been hard to get any information from. They don't like the Americans."

She said it casually, as if it didn't matter.

"We had a number of soldiers in America once. When the war ended, many of the soldiers wanted to go home. But processing was slow, and they all went to England first. Many stayed there for more than eighteen months before they went back to their homeland."

He nodded. The pounding in his chest grew harder, until the pulsing beat throbbed in his ears. So loud he did not hear her at first when she asked him what he wanted to find.

"I want to look up a place," he said quietly.

"Town?" she said and patted the desk impatiently to get his attention.

"Elenruhe. I am sorry," he apologized. She pulled a large binder from a shelf and opened it to an indexed page, running her finger along the list. On the other side of the desk, Jan read along with her, above and upside down.

"Yes, well, we have no records of survivors from that town." She shut the book and raised her head to look at him, frowning at the lack of name. She turned and pulled another book out of a shelf. This time her finger found its mark halfway through the names. Jan's hand tightened on his cap, *Elenruhe, home, Eve and Pieter.*

Each second seemed an hour long and the pounding filled his ears once more. He turned to look at the shelves behind him, if he knew which one he would go to it. He did not have her patience. Still she didn't move to find anything and he looked straight into her face.

"That town," she said, "was bombed when we took Germany at the end."

He listened, not wanting to hear the words. They grew faint as she kept on speaking.

"We have the Movietone footage that was taken on file." She looked at him doubtfully. "Would you be wanting to see that?"

His stomach clutched. *Want to, no, but I must.*

"Yes." He was careful to use the American word.

Still looking doubtful, she moved to a shelf and took a film spool from a metal box. She fitted it to a projector in the very back of the office, then moved to answer the phone, which was ringing without stop.

He sat in the darkened room and tried to see the film on the screen as home. The grainy sepia figures jerked and hurried in a macabre acting out of the narrator's frenzied words.

And then he watched the planes swoop down, their shadows racing along the ground far below, wavering and foreshortening as they crossed over ponds and roads and fences. And houses. And people.

He took a deep breath. *This was his town.* The hill with the long road winding down to meet the train track that ran along the wider south road. The camera got closer; that meant the plane was getting closer.

Closer. Closer. He gripped the table edge. It was a race to get there first.

The buildings grew in detail. The bread shop, the pharmacy, the train station. And next to the train station was a small, square building with a long terrace at one end.

The film made a sudden hop.

"Oops." The Red Cross woman was back. She flipped a switch and eased the film a bit. "There's a splice there where they ran two cameras' film together. The first focus got lost when the plane's bombs exploded really close, I'd bet. The air shock would have sent the plane up a good bit.

"One camera would do wide, you know, panoramic shots. The other did more close up. They studied those for which buildings were the factories."

Jan stared straight ahead.

The librarian reeled on, fascinated with her own voice and the details. Admiring the thought and preparation that went into the killing they were about to see.

He felt sweat prickle in his hairline. "Then the rest of this film will be closer up?"

"Yes. There." She restarted the film, and the train station gave a sudden lurch, like a thing suddenly unfrozen. The small terrace loomed; it was his house in sudden detail. Smoke from bombs and dust wafted and wreathed around it. There were still flowers in the window boxes. He looked closer. Geraniums. Eve's favorite.

Now the flowers waved madly in a wind he could not feel from this safe seat miles and years away.

The crackle of bombs and machine guns sounded abruptly. Then the walls of his home blew outward, and in almost slow motion the bricks lifted gracefully into the air and settled back onto themselves in a pile pierced by jagged pieces of beam and roof.

"Enough." He got the word out, forcing it from his throat. "I've seen enough."

The woman obligingly off turned the projector off. He struggled for a moment and willed that he would not throw up on her feet.

"So much hatred," she murmured as she put away the film. "Those Germans are a troubled people. These deaths bother me more. They were not like the soldiers, fighting for something. They were women and children."

She looked out of the window at the bricked street full of old-fashioned shops and flowers. The sight of a town living a gray, rainy afternoon, filled with bright spots of color as people hurried from shop to shop.

"That main street didn't look too much different from this one, before that day." She nodded at the film. "But then again, such a picturesque place bred those awful monsters. Evil can wear many faces. I expect that is why it is so hard to see it coming." She shuffled her papers together and asked him briskly, "Is there anything else I can find for you?"

"There are no other records?" He tried one last time, not wanting the flickering, jagged film to be all that anyone ever saw of a place he had loved so much.

"No, not that I know of. We can send a request to the International Red Cross office and they can look for us. Would you like for me to do that?" She took up a pen and paper. "I'll need your name and address."

Icy fingers twisted Jan's intestines into a sharp ball.

He could not give his name.

Better not to ask again, he decided. *To do so will bring notice to me.*

He answered that there was nothing else, that he had just been curious. She put the reel away in the dark vault with short, sharp motions of impatience, as if she were punishing the reel for existing, for the stupidity of the jerky figures on the screen.

Jan got his coat and started to slip it on, then dropped his cap on the floor. As he rose from picking it up, the thin woman said, "I hate what they have done, destroying decency for all of us."

She turned and walked away between the quiet, high shelves, and he took a last look around. It would not be possible to come here again. It would not be safe in this freest of countries. He might be free to be different and ask questions, but others were free to notice and wonder. And that might get him found out.

There was no reason for that now, not with Eve and the baby dead. He wondered if in so much destruction, if bodies would ever be found, even looked for.

He caught the local bus for the Cape.

"How was your day?" Emmett greeted him at home in Rachel's Corner. Dinner was ready, thick clam chowder simmered with onions and potatoes.

"I saw much," Jan answered him. "It is a big city with people going everywhere."

"Want to live there?" Emmett asked him.

"No, no, too many places to go," Jan answered him, staring at the heavy chowder. *And none of them are mine. There is no place left in the world for me. I am not even me anymore.*

Abruptly he put down his bowl and said, "Will you excuse me for the night? I am more tired than I thought." He rose and went to his small room, crawled beneath the blankets and lay staring at the ceiling, seeing faces and past times in the dark stain above his head.

In the months after, Jan decided that hell was to know you had been a monster who started the machine in motion that went on to kill those you loved most.

His favorite moment of the day was when the sun just began to silver the flooded bogs with faint light. He would stand on the edge and watch it come. Before his trip to Boston, it had been his most peaceful moment of the day, but now his thoughts would go back to the dying of so many people.

Somehow, before, he had put it away from him, but now the thoughts came to stand and look back at him, shadows among the still dark trees along the water's edge.

But he kept rising, going about the early chores in the gray half-light of dawn. There was always much preparation work before the next harvest would begin.

The evenings by the fire fell into a routine of dinner and reading and bed.

Emmet died in the spring of 1959, as quietly as he had lived. That winter Jan had carried him easily to the dark, cool barn to check on the cranberries curing there or the horses waiting patiently in their stalls.

He left everything to Jan. "Such as it is," he said, with no quiver in his voice. "It's my time, I expect."

Jan buried him as he asked and went home to the small, shingled house and waited for the bogs to need him, for the season to begin.

But then the bleeding started to worsen. At first, he didn't know why. He visited Dr. Hemshaw, the lean and grizzled town physician who fished as much as he practiced medicine.

A new young man, Will Sustine, had joined the practice. A stocky, bluff man new to the town, he did not talk much and questioned less.

Will Sustine took time, though, looking Jan over thoroughly. The muscle tone had been good for years and the skin healthy and tight. What bothered him most were the eyes and ears, and the bleeding.

He ran his hand over the strange, blued lump on the underside of Jan's arm. Hard, fibrous, he would watch it in the years to come.

"Does that hurt?" Sustine squeezed it in between thumb and forefinger. One end of it looked like the tag end of a number, the last part of maybe an eight, but how would a number get beneath the skin?

"No, not anymore," Jan answered without thinking.

"Did it once?" Hemshaw asked.

"No, not really." Jan shook his head. "I can not even really remember when it happened."

That part was true enough, about the scarring. It had been a gradual thing. He had memories of sitting fireside on a low stool after Emmet died and he lived alone. Arm raised, the light flickering and bouncing off the soft inside of his forearm. He worked with a syringe and needle, injecting bleach beneath his skin, almost passing out from the burning as the caustic liquid made contact.

Each time took such a little bit of the number away, sometimes he thought that he would never finish. He drank to dull the burning. At last, one by one, the numbers and letters had melted into one hard lump of ink as the bleach weakened and destroyed all the tissue beneath the skin.

It hardened into a scar until it became a blue infused lump of tissue that felt like wood lodged beneath the skin.

"No," he said again. "That has been there for a while. It does not trouble me."

Sustine dropped the arm, "Well, Jan, I can't find an answer. We've tried the usual things for allergies and weaknesses... I think you've just got something from long ago catching up with you now." He sighed and switched off the bright bulb of his scope.

"It's a bit funny, as though your body just gets too hot for itself. But maybe we will find an answer someday."

Jan asked himself, *would then my heart quit hurting?*

Cape Cod, 1975, Found

Bleeding became a part of the day, worsening when he worked hard. Or when he ran, like he did that day when the Air Force man caught him again at the tunnels. He went as fast as he could, but his feet seemed to move oh-so-slowly across the pine needle carpet. His vision swam and the trees wavered in a chorus line dance of their own.

Come on, he thought he heard the branches beckon, *one more step toward us.*

Then there was nothing.

He came to on the ground in a pool of his own blood with a man bending over him.

Rankin, M. the nametag read.

They had gone to Will Sustine.

Chapter 24

Return to 1996

J an's words slowed and we drifted back into 1996. The tide of memory spread out like a stream that has gone to sea, no longer bound by the narrow channels that tumble and speed along a river's flow.

Outside, the Cape was waking into day, and in the grate the fire popped gently, sending welcome fingers of warmth against my bare legs. Even in summer, ocean mornings can hold a chill.

I didn't remember any of us rising to light the fire, but realized when I tried to move how long we had been sitting. I unlimbered slowly, protests shooting through my limbs as I did so.

"You will stay here and sleep?" Jan asked, for we had listened the whole night long. He probably meant all of us, but his eyes only saw Pieter. Pieter sat silent for so long that I almost nudged him except for Cameron's discouraging me with a slight headshake.

"No," Pieter said at last. "Tonight, last night, has been so full that I need to let it settle a bit. And I do not think I can do that here. Not right now, anyway." He looked at Cameron and me. "I'll go back with you, if you don't mind."

"Sure," said Cameron easily and bent to find his shoes. I sat quietly, not sure if Pieter meant returning to the inn or the whole way back home. Our stories weren't even the same anymore.

Leaving was right, though. I wanted to sit and watch the ocean, the waves rolling in, blue-white in the newlit morning and think about this side of my father that I never suspected. We rose and murmured good-byes and drove back toward the inn. No one spoke. I thought of a shower and crisp sheets and listened to the hum of the tires on the road as we drove. Just then, it seemed enough.

But once I was in bed, sleep would not come, though the thoughts did thick and fast, pondering the mystery of Matthew and Jan crossing paths, how Pieter came to follow them.

I rose after an hour, made coffee and sat on the balcony, watching the bay dotted with small bits of color and bright, mid-morning light. I wanted to be out in it, sloshing my feet in the riffle of waves just touching the shore.

In the mirror I looked drowsy and slow, despite my inner restlessness. I freshened my cup of coffee and slipped back outside. Pieter's room was quiet, too, the shut door and drawn blinds keeping him safe within. I imagined him lying taut and awake in the dimness, ginned with the same energy as me.

We had arrived here focused on our fathers, bound by that goal and prospect. From here on, we would be our separate selves again.

The screen door slid open behind me and Cameron emerged.

"Not sleepy?" he asked.

"No, tired, but not sleepy," I agreed. "It's been a lot to listen to."

He came and stood next to me, rubbing the back of my neck gently. I sighed.

"Time to go home," I said.

"Yes," he said against my hair. "I'm ready, too."

We finished our coffee, and I went in and called the airport. Yes, seats were available on the next day's flight, and I booked two seats all the way home.

"I'll shower," Cameron said, "You go on down and walk on the beach if you want. We'll have to tell Pieter and his father that we are going, but perhaps that's good. We need to leave them to it."

I nodded, relieved. I padded barefoot down the stairs to the beach. I felt light, buoyed to be headed home, as though the wind could take me if I let it. The sand was warm under my feet as I stepped from the bottom stair onto the beach.

I walked to the water's edge, where it was firm under my feet. There I only left the barest of footprints, and the surf swirled in right behind me, smoothing away each trace of my steps.

I picked my way through the rocks and rounded the last one to find Pieter on the beach, pants rolled up against the tide, coffee in hand.

"Good morning," he said. "You could not sleep either?"

"No," I said. "I thought you were, though. Sleeping."

He shook his head. "I need to move about."

We turned and walked toward Falmouth in the distance, damp, salty sand clinging to our toes.

Pieter sipped coffee silently. I thought how much of him I had come to know, how much of me he seemed to see. Next to me, he stopped suddenly, looking past me, a faint sheen of tears in his blue, blue eyes.

In that teeny space of time, my heart's door opened just a crack. I realized I had not even known that it had been closed. Something inside me squeezed tight, way down deep, all the way through the muscle and into the soul beyond. I had had a father to lose.

The day that Matthew died, I became sure the heart and soul share breath and space until that final last divide. I am also certain that some hearts share a bit of each other.

Memories, at the very best, those will only ever be bits and pieces of a world that was, a place and time gone by. It is what we do with the pieces of now, the parts of us we find, that counts.

Who would Pieter become? I looked at those blue, blue eyes, so like a piece of the sky. So like his father's as well.

"What will you do now?" I asked him to spur time back into its normal rhythm.

"I am going to stay," he said. "For a while."

"Are you?" I was surprised. "I didn't feel you would last night."

"Well, Germans do not decide fast. But this morning it is clear that is what it is to do." He smiled slightly and looked around.

He gestured toward Jan's place in the pines just visible across the bay. "I should get to know him in his place."

Behind me, the trees of Rachel's Corner sighed with the late morning breeze and I thought that there were worse places to be.

"Then, perhaps, we will go back and see some of over there. For now, here is enough. Neither of us is the same anymore, the person we used to be."

I liked thinking of them here on this beach. In all this unsettledness, I liked knowing where things belonged, liked to be sure they were in their place. Though I was not as sure as I once would've been of where those places are. *Perhaps we are better off*, I thought, *if we mostly just try to make our own place and let others do the same.*

"There is work to do here, also," he said, and I realized he had been speaking. I paid attention again to his words. "I would not be happy, I do not think, without some work to do. And it is the kind of work that will tire a man. A good tired."

I looked across the bay with him and saw sun and sea and a small house tucked in its trees, a picturesque, ordinary place for such extraordinary events.

"I don't know, I don't think I will call him Papa." Pieter smiled, and the very air around us seemed to lighten. "Somehow that seems too much to try for at more than fifty."

"Then again, this whole long connection is pretty hard to believe. And it turned out to be true," I said. "Maybe it would be best just to see what comes."

"Yes, that is so. I will be here for a time. Something for the mind and something for the heart. Not bad, almost a balance." He smiled again.

Cameron came towards us, kicking through the sand, eyes cast down in one last beachcombing journey, looking for things left along the shore by the ocean and by man.

Maybe left either way, by fate, a thing we cannot see until we are upon it.

Headed Home

We sat in the airport at sunrise the next morning, waiting for our hopper flight. As we sipped a last coffee and watched a red carpet of sun rays roll across the waves, a hand fell onto my shoulder.

I turned to find Jan at my side and Pieter standing just behind him. A son new to his role.

"Your carpet home, they are welcoming you," Jan said with a gesture at the brilliant path. Though it went east, not west, as we would travel, I understood. I smiled. I was surprised they had come. It was probably the first time Jan had been in a crowded place on purpose in more than twenty years.

A hum and the crackle of static sounded as our flight was called. A sudden flurry of newspapers, bags and books brought a crowd to the gate. We stood for a moment, unsure, all of us feeling it had all been said. I wondered if anyone else knew who this old man was, even if Jan did himself.

If and when he went home with Pieter, what would people see? A Nazi going home, a man returning to himself, a father going to learn about his son?

All of these in whole and part. Would anyone care at all if they knew the secrets that he held? Or would they say, that is all yesterday, ancient history. Let's go see a movie?

I shouldered my bag, and Cameron flipped once more through our ticket folders to make sure all was in order. Jan raised a hand; behind him Pieter bowed his head in my direction. Another soldier's child who had learned not to say too much.

"See ya," Jan said. We touched hands lightly, as though too much would fray the moment.

"See ya," I answered. The ground I stood on was not so steady beneath my feet to be ready for those words.

Jan said, "I want you to know that I will not forget. That it will stay important to me, the things that you have done."

My throat grew tight with tears I would not cry. Soldiers' daughters don't do that either.

When we lifted off the Hyannis runway and circled out over the ocean to head south and home, I leaned forward to watch the Cape fall away. Out to sea, a wall of mist lay low on the water, the first fingers of gray already creeping to shore. By noon, they would be socked with the next storm of the season.

It was easy to picture Pieter and Jan walking in the foggy, silent wetness of trees and trails, or listening on the beach to the slap of wave on rocks they could not see. Things are kinder in gentle light, and they had much to discover that a softening of edges could ease.

But that was not my place, and it was good when the wing banked above me and we headed for the mainland. From Boston we had a direct flight home, but a four-hour wait until then. By the time we landed back in Texas, the sun would be on its way down, having been beside us all day. I wanted to be home to hear, in the days to come, Linnea and Leah playing among the trees above the creek, to sip wine and plan what to put in my attic.

Now that the secrets were gone, there was empty space to fill.

The flight was lightly booked and we moved into the window and aisle seats so we could spread out and sleep as we flew. Riding in the empty seat between us were the wraiths of a crew of people no longer here, a bit of Matthew and Jan and Pieter and the people Cameron and I had been before we took this trip.

Cameron slept the whole trip. I stared out the window and thought, of buildings and bombs and airplanes and the soldiers who manned them. I had seen the results of war, the taking apart of one life so that others were made from the pieces and lived along these new edges and shapes. Lives we might not have expected, but that we must live out once we were in them.

I tried to think of what Matthew and Jan and Pieter had most in common, and the word that whispered itself again and again was bravery.

There is a question that if a tree falls in the forest and no one is there to hear it, does it make a sound? Or does it fall in silence? I think sometimes the bravest things are the ones that happen in silence. An accolade, being heard, is just a reflection of what was. It does not change the heart of what can be chosen. So, yes, bravery can happen in silence. But what kind of bravery do we mean? What scariness does each of us face?

For Matthew, what could be braver than being yourself in the face of a world that chooses to go another way? Matthew walked away from a career that might have arced even higher, like fireworks in the night. He took what he knew and saw and decided for himself what felt right. I wish I had known. I wish I could have told him how proud I was of his choice.

For Jan, he who was Franz, it was the specter of himself that drew him into night wakings and musings and quiet times by a fire trying hard not to think of a life that wasn't anymore. Can there be a harder task than to see a monster in a mirror and know it is yourself?

Yes, a task harder still, and one that he had mastered, was to tame that beast, to face squarely the regret within himself, and to live with that and truly wish it had not been so.

And Pieter? Well, Pieter had fought the battle many of us do, discovering that the scariest thing is the thing we do not know. He took a chance bit of learning and turned it into a man, a father: his. I thought about how hard it must have been to come looking, to tell Cameron and me his fantastic-seeming tale and to go with us to find the ending.

I wondered if I would not have stopped upon reading the end of the journal, letting the finish write itself in some comfortable fabled way, like a prince in a German castle high on a cliff. Like the story Pieter's oma told about the princess that he likened to his mother. Only to be found in a story.

I sighed loudly, and Cameron stirred beside me, waking to see the sunset out the plane window. He reached for my hand and lapsed back into drowsing with a lazy smile.

At peace, with me, Cameron was headed home. I sighed again, and this time he did not stir. I was glad; it would not help to talk and, even though I loved him, there was one part of this I must do and do alone. I still had to say good-bye to Matthew. A lump lodged in my throat and tears prickled, yet did not fall. Tomorrow, I thought, like Scarlett O'Hara, tomorrow was another day.

Matthew's Graveside, One More Time

I chose a morning to go to the cemetery when it was dark and windy, the kind of day when you could not judge the time from light or sun or shadow. The sky was heavy with gathering storm, but it wouldn't rain for a while, I thought, and I hurried to gather purse and keys and shoes. I headed out the door and across town in the morning traffic.

Assumption Cemetery, where Matthew lies, is old, the oldest burying ground in town. Once beyond the bustle of houses and roads, now it is hemmed in by tall buildings with many window-eyes and a double-decker freeway.

Above and behind me, the highway thundered with people driving to work, to town, to living. It struck me as an odd juncture, this place of sleeping right next to the rumbling, racing road. But, of course, that happens with cemeteries that come from the past, like this one.

It was hard to imagine anyone resting in eternity with such commotion going on.

I slowed for the entrance and saw, inside the fence, tall, green trees and the two dirt roads that wandered through all the graves, an island of stillness in the morning rush.

I braked for the pothole in the drive between the red brick pillars that lean slightly, after all these years. Just as I eased forward, a single raindrop fell with a loud splat right in the middle of the windshield.

I stopped hard then, halfway through the gate and waited for any more rain. But the one drop was by itself, and above me the gray was torn and showing blue.

I stared at the one drop and knew with certainty that I was not alone. A sudden lightness filled me. The earth smelled rich and fresh; the wind blew, and leaves scattered.

I stopped my car on the caliche road next to our plot and turned off the motor. Streaks of sun fell through a jumble of red oaks that stood watch above the cemetery, slanting over my shoulder to the piece of ground I'd come to touch.

It would be hard to find a more Texas place, and I thought Matthew would have liked that. A pecan tree soared overhead, breaking the sun and heat already summing itself to chase off the coolness of early morning.

I gathered my flowers from the front seat and swung the car door open. I'd ended up with a mixed bouquet, unable to settle on one kind. I was just learning to say good-bye, and I'd taken a long time trying to decide which flowers held the message. At length I'd decided that one kind would not do, not right now.

I sat for a moment and smelled the fresh sweetness wafting from the bunch in my hands.

I got out and rounded the car to read the marker placed at the base of the tree. *Matthew J. Rankin, Colonel, United States Air Force*. He faced west, with a view of the city and the sunsets.

He would like that, keeping an eye on those in motion and knowing when the day is done.

This marker startled me still, and I reached for the thoughts I had gathered in another bout of two a.m. musings, but instead realized that Matthew already knew.

The volleys in honor of bravery had been fired, the words spoken of rest and peace and honor and wishes, long before this day.

By everyone but me.

It was time for the grief to be past, time for the lesson and remembrance to be part of the present I make. I found a symmetry in his dying on the Fourth of July, as though the fathers of this country had called him home at the very moment his choosing might be noticed by someone. Someone.

For me there was still a question of things I could not see, but peace stole in at this moment, my own little island of it, and I realized I had gotten an answer to some of those things I didn't know. I had a better sense now of the man who raised me, knew something of his character and his past.

The little flag on his grave snapped at my feet in a sudden gust of breeze, tiny and bright, a colorful reminder of always standing straight and true.

What I liked best was that Matthew had done this all unknown. Not living for rules nor ribbons nor retribution. That he had done it in silence made me admire him, made me think more of Matthew as a man than as an officer. And they are quite different things.

I liked that he just did it for the reason that he thought it right. No more, no less, no other. It made me have a sense of the man inside the quietness, the rules of army, the role of parenting. It told me something of Matthew himself. I wished we had talked. But at least I admired what I knew, and it made his passing more a step of a lifetime rather than the end of one.

A girl in a man's world is how I looked back on my growing up time. I had often felt trapped by Matthew's expectations of me. Some were of me and some were for me, but they were all many steps ahead of wherever I was at that time.

Matthew didn't make clear how and where they were to be reached, and so the path to getting there was often not easily found. It came from my own reckoning and choosing. My own mind and my own invention found trails and ways far different from those he would have carved across whatever wilderness he faced, whichever mountain he climbed.

I thought Matthew made a good soldier because it was a tough and ready thing. You do it, kill it, bomb it, eat it. But speaking, acknowledging love and thought were not a part of the moment and so had never been part of the past.

I was probably the only mountain Matthew never conquered. The more he ordered and shoved and punished, the more internal I became, the less it mattered to me what rule was broken. I behaved according to myself.

Still, what Matthew never knew was how hard I tried to fit into his world. How much the toughness cost me, not being able to say I cared. For to care in Matthew's world was, as far as I knew, a weakness.

Then Pieter brought this story, this picture, and we began to look for Jan.

I looked in the mirror that very morning, as the steam from my shower cleared, and I searched for what Matthew saw in me that made me the one he set the task of finding out. He must have seen something, or he would not have left me with this charge.

He did not have to leave the objects in the attic, but I think he wanted someone to know. Someone to say what happened.

I thought back to the beach, to the ocean, to the water that touched the other side; a land where lives were lived, wars fought, and people died. Once it seemed like those days were long ago and had nothing to do with now, but it was not so.

All days have to do with each other. What we do with our gifts of time forever touches something else.

There are rooms that exist even though no one will say so, so hidden are the entries. Some of these are secret chambers of the heart, some are alcoves and corners of the mind and some are real and dusty places with hidden, hard–to-find doors.

Whether guarded by cobwebs, spells or laser beams and keypad touches, they are there - have been, through history up to now.

Into such a room, that doesn't exist, mind you, went the proof of who Jan was, the record of accidental poisonings and a little book with some writing in it that almost told what my father knew. A question remained of what all Matthew knew.

As was the question of who was my father, really? But do any of us in the role of parent or child, ever fully know that answer?

I thought I knew from all this searching what kind of man he tried to be. And that perhaps, was the boiled down, distilled, strained-through-cheesecloth truth that all of us want.

I could see Matthew caught between the oath to his country and the dawning realization of unnecessary lives destroyed in the terribleness of war.

Matthew was a soldier through and through. At least at first he was. I think he was more a man when his own thoughts became his guide. I did not know when he died that saying good-bye was so important. But it was - and even more for me, I needed to know whom I was saying goodbye to.

This day, the pecan leaves rained down, rustling about me as the wind came up and the sun arced toward noon to meet it. I had gained a picture of the man who had been my father. Of the man that Matthew was. And the person who was me.

Matthew did what he thought was right - sometimes that is the same as for your country, sometimes it is not. Matthew's mother, grandmother and aunt lie here too. I broke the bouquet and placed a carnation on each of their graves as well.

I thought for a moment of what to say, but instead realized that Matthew already knew. What I'd been missing was that he was waiting for me to know it too. He had been restless for me to know him enough that I could let him go.

I sighed and stepped forward. And I said the final words, the ones I knew he wanted to hear from me, those of the trying times when his efforts to bridge our distances I saw as something to scramble over, instead of something to lean on.

"See ya, "I murmured softly, and laid the remaining jumble of color across the middle, the heart, of Matthew's resting place and stood for just a moment longer. Hot tears came then, and the flowers blurred and wheeled until I did not see them anymore.

And then both the wind and I were silent.

A bird twittered in the moment's sudden hush, and I had a feeling I had indeed been heard. And answered. It was said and done for then. Some ghosts had been lain to rest, both here and yonder.

I gathered myself and my things about me.

Then I went on home.

About the Author

Cheryl Kerr grew up in both civilian and military settings. She has published fiction and nonfiction. See Ya is her second novel. She lives in the Texas Hill Country with her family and a horse named Hallelujah.